Heath,
Hope u
enjoy!
Brighty
Jeremy!

Love,
U

Shot
By Lexi Ostrow

Dedicated to the men and women in blue who protect our cities. To all the lives that have been lost in the line of duty, and all the families left to pick up the pieces.

PROLOGUE

She had been shot. There were no ifs, ands, or buts about it. She was going down.

She could feel herself dropping to the ground, could feel the slide of her blood as it ran down her abdomen and shoulder. She had let her partner down – let the love of her life down. Now, they were very much alone.

She felt her body sink to the ground. There was nothing left. Nothing, but her pain, failure, and the ground to catch her as she waited for help to come.

Six months prior

Trevor clenched his jaw and his fists at the same time. Five hundred and ninety-seven days locked up, and they were now letting him go for good behavior.

For five hundred and ninety-seven days, he'd rotted in a jail cell after being caught by cops from the various branches of Southern California's police departments that never should have been working together in the first place.

Five hundred and ninety-seven days he'd spent on crappy food and dodging knives thrown by jackasses who thought they were better than him and could make him their bitch.

Five hundred and ninety-seven days stuck in jail, and four hundred of them spent pretending he was something other than what he was. Four hundred of those days acting as like some repenting little snot who felt guilty about being caught in an armed robbery and accidentally shooting a cop. It had been an accident, but no one had believed him.

It had worked, though. Once every year, he was brought up for parole. Finally, after snitching on at least six other inmates, he'd finally gotten what he wanted.

Freedom.

The freedom to take down every single police station that had a hand in his arrest. Had a hand in the five hundred and ninety-seven days he'd spent rotting in jail because his partners had all bailed from the scene of the crime. Well, almost all. He hadn't been locked up alone, but it hardly mattered to Trevor.

The bright light of the sun flashed in his eyes as the police officer pushed open the San Diego Police Department's doors. He flinched at the sudden assault of sun and shivered as the cool November air raced over his skin. It felt good to feel cold. It felt good to feel anything real at all.

He was going to feel, all right. He and his old friends were about to have a little reunion and play a game. One where the only option was going to be to play on his side, or learn first hand just how much he'd learned from the scum in prison who'd helped him come up with enough strategy to take down officers from the state's finest precincts before retiring someplace even warmer than sunny Southern California.

A grin stretched across his lips. Trevor nodded as the officer removed his cuffs for the last time. He let the pretense drop, the light in his eyes went dead as he thought about the police officers he intended to hunt.

Bridget's hips swayed seductively back and forth as the beat from the music coursed through her body. Her now short black hair swished across her ears, and she let her hands wave in the air alongside her friend's. Tonight was her last night partying and drinking like a model. Tomorrow morning, she'd report for her first day as a police recruit at the Los Angeles Police Department.

She ran her hands down her body as the music slipped into a sinful Rihanna song. Bridget walked off the dance floor to grab a drink. Her head already swam from the amount of shots she'd consumed with the girls from her agency. One of her three inch silver heels stuck to a slosh of drying alcohol. She tipped forward, her hand landing squarely on someone's back. The girl gave her a dirty look. Bridget waved it off and continued to the bar.

"One shot of Patron," she shouted over the music as she finally got to the counter and tapped her hand across the counter to a song she'd never heard before as she waited.

A shot appeared in front of her. The scantily clad bartender smiled at her.

"Eight-fifty."

Bridget scoffed and fumbled to grab her card from her sparkling clutch. She passed it to the other woman as she tipped her head back and let the vile alcohol slide down her throat just in time to grab her card. She didn't sign the slip or tip. She'd been drinking all night and they no longer needed her generous tips. Besides, police weren't paid as well as models.

She stepped to the side and looked out over the club. It was too crowded for a Sunday night, but it was Los Angeles. Tonight would be the last night she would likely indulge this way. Cops weren't known for their partying and truth be told, it was the excuse she needed to put this life behind her. It was never the life she'd wanted anyway.

Her father had been a homicide detective since before she had been born. Every story he had ever told had fascinated her. Dealing with the bad guys, helping those that needed it, and solving crimes had been her bedtime stories. It may have been where her father went wrong, because when she was seventeen, she'd told him she didn't want to go to college. . She wanted to be a cop instead.

His refusal to accept it, or even allow it, had been a source of contempt between them, but in the end, she had gone to USC for Criminal Investigation to appease her father because he had been her whole world. Disappointing him would have been akin to killing him. She'd always thought she would be able to convince him she could handle herself as a cop and still walk in his footsteps when college was over.

She'd been twenty when she'd driven her car into the backend of a talent scout scout's vehicle. Three weeks and a massive ticket her father couldn't get waived later, she'd signed a contract with American Model Management and moved to New York. She'd finished school through a series of online classes and had been living the glamorous life ever since. Bridget had never completely gelled with it, however, staying away from the drugs and constant partying.

She had enjoyed more than her fair share of the riches the lifestyle offered, including her loft on the Upper East Side. Until twelve weeks ago, when her mother had called her. The distress in her mother's voice had tipped her off before the words had been out of her mother's mouth. Her father had been murdered. Shot down right outside the bar he and his old cop friends used to hang out in during their retirement.

The time between then and now was a blur to Bridget. So much had happened so quickly. She'd paid her way out of her contract, leaving her with enough for a few months rent. Bridget had then moved back home. She hadn't wanted to do anything except make sure her father's killer was caught, arrested and hopefully put in jail with a life sentence for killing an ex-cop hanging over his head. The Los Angeles Police were hiring, and thanks to her father's twenty-three years on the force, she'd been a quick selection for the academy.

Which meant tonight, she would say said goodbye to being a carefree thirty-one- year -old, and hello to the life she'd always wanted. It just hurt to know that she was only here because she'd wanted to honor her father; that he would never see her graduate from training or have the late night talks she'd always dreamt of with him. She should have had the guts to walk away from modeling long ago and do something to help people like she'd always wanted.

"It's not about you, Bridget. It's about being someone your dad would've been proud of." She clenched her fists and shook her head. There wasn't enough alcohol in her system if she was having these thoughts. "And there's not enough money in your bank account to load up on any more,"

She sighed and turned back to the bar. One more shot and then she'd lose herself in the oblivion of a night of dancing. At least until two am, when she promised herself she would leave.

The bartender raised a brow but said nothing. "Need another?"

Bridget nodded, passed her card, and felt a large hand lay on top of hers.

"I'll take care of hers."

The most sensuous deep southern accent she'd ever heard drifted down to her. She turned around to give the man a piece of her mind. Her retort was promptly silenced when she whirled about to face him. The man who'd offered to buy her a drink was stunning. She was used to hot men from the shoots she'd done in the past, but this man put them all to shame.

He towered over her, standing at about six-feet-two inches tall. His whole body was muscled and she swore he was the size of a house. Chiseled cheekbones, a classically straight nose, and a small side smirk sent a rush of desire through her entire body. His hair was perfectly coiffed, a deep chestnut brown that matched the straight slash of brows over his bright blue eyes.

"Thanks."

Her tongue felt thick as she said the words and continued to look him over. She wasn't one to hop into bed with a stranger, but if this particular one asked her to, she wouldn't argue. He took his own drink as she picked up hers his smirk changed subtly into a devilish smile as he lifted the small shot glass towards her.

"Cheers."

He tipped his head back. She watched as the chorded muscles in his neck rolled as he swallowed his drink. Slightly mesmerized, she tossed back the shot of Patron and choked a little at the burn she hadn't prepped for. His laughing response was deep, and sinful thoughts tweaked inside her mind.

Tonight had been about fun with her high school pals and a few of the girls who'd flown in to see her. Not a night for hooking up with incredibly beautiful men.

"Plans change," she muttered to herself and smiled up at him. "So who do I have to thank for that shot?" Coyly, she raised a brow and wondered if she even needed to employ any sort of technique as he'd already randomly purchased a drink for her.

He pointed upward and spun his index finger around. "Too damned loud in here. Care to join me out on the patio?"

His voice was more drowned out as they walked away from the bar. Several seconds later, but she froze. Going places with strange men was a part of who she'd been, not who she was going to be, Bridget O'Casey, LAPD. Her pulse pounded as she thought the offer over. Going out onto the equally crowded, but much quieter, patio wasn't going to get her killed.

She did want to get to know him better, and this was a fantastic way to justify her actions if she wound up in his bed come morning.

She nibbled on her lower lip and shrugged. Bridget's eyes landed on one of the girl's who'd come with her. Her friend gave her a thumbs up. Being a cop's daughter made her cautious about everything but her friend's approval eased her a little. For this one night, though, she'd give it up for a little fun.

"That would be great," she shouted over the uproar as Lady Gaga's most recent song blasted through the club.

His large hand wrapped around her slender one, and she shivered from the contact. He was warm, not sweaty warm, just warm. She allowed him to pull her through the crowded room of sparkling and sweaty streaked bodies. Bridget shivered as the cold November air raced across her exposed skin when he pushed open the door.

The noise level dropped significantly. She was secretly glad that it meant she'd be able to better hear his southern accent. Her eyes dropped to watch his backside as he tugged her rather skillfully over to a small, green wrought iron table and chair set.

"It's a shame we can't get some more drinks out here," he said with a smile on his lips as she sat down. "Let's try this again. Jeremy Trellins, nice to meet you."

The way the deep timbre of his voice slid over her senses was enough to make her shiver with anticipation of what other things he might say to her. Slowly, she extended her hand and he took it.

"Bridget O'Casey."

She shifted in her chair, noticing how slick with sweat her silver stretch-knit dress was, suddenly wishing she'd worn something that breathed a lot better. Bridget fought back a gasp at the lack of contact when he let go of her hand and leaned back into her chair.

"So, Jeremy Trellins, how many women have you bought drinks for tonight?"

Her tone was playful. She winked at him. Deep down, she was curious about how many rungs she would mark on his bedpost if he managed to seduce her. Which, given his voice and looks, wouldn't take too much convincing, since she was certainly interested.

He laughed and she watched as two dimples formed on each side of his mouth. His smile deepened and he became that much more handsome than moments before. He raised his arms up in fake surrender and slowed his laughter down.

"You've got me. I'm not the slickest at this."

She raised a brow at him. "Oh, really? So, what number, Mr. Trellins?"

He grinned and she felt her stomach do a little flip and heat raced through her body. A smile like that would get anyone into bed, it didn't matter what else they did or didn't know about him.

"First one of the evening." He winked this time, and she laughed.

"Really now? First one tonight? I feel pretty honored."

She flashed him a smile and sub consciously told herself to tone it down. She'd never done this particular thing before. If she wasn't careful, she'd come across like an idiot.

"I don't make it a habit of buying pretty ladies drinks. Don't make it a habit to come to clubs, really."

He leaned back in the chair and she watched the muscles in his arms flex as they rested on the arm rests. This man was getting more and more intriguing, and she'd only known him for five minutes.

"What's the occasion?"

She watched as an emotion flickered across his face before as he hesitated to answer.

"Finished something I was working on. Big time stuff. My buddies wanted to take me out to celebrate. Sooner or later, they'll think I've gone home when they don't see me inside."

Heat curled into a ball inside her stomach and she swallowed, trying to discern any hidden meaning behind his words.

"Well then, I'll consider myself very fortunate, Mr. Trellins."

He His face flushed with color, and she drooled over him even more. A man who looked like that and was humble, she was beginning to think her father had somehow been looking out for her tonight.

"Call me Jeremy, please. I have to hear my last name at work all day. It's a nice change to have someone use my first."

She smiled and leaned forward in her chair. Reaching across the small table, she gently pressed her palm to his forearm.

"Well then, Jeremy. I believe I owe you a thank you."

She rose out of the seat and placed a soft kiss on his left cheek before sitting back down. Bridget had no idea if the action got his blood pumping as fast as it did hers, but she did see the way his eyes darkened as they stared at one another.

"The pleasure is all mine, Bridget."

The words sounded low and sultry. She couldn't help but hope they held a promise of more to come.

**

Bridget laughed as Jeremy's hands fumbled to pull the keys out of the ignition of his 2010 Camaro. She couldn't help but feel some of the sexual tension in the car rise a notch. She heard the clang as they dropped out of his hands onto the floor, taking and she took off her seatbelt and as she climbed out of the yellow sports car.

"I swear, I'm not typically clumsy. About anything."

His eyes found hers and she shivered with excitement.

They'd spent the better part of an hour outside on the patio before he'd asked her to dance. One simple question and her body had made up its mind about where they would be going after the club. On the dance floor his hands had trailed a sensual path down the curves of her body, and she'd found herself leaning backward against him. Their bodies had swayed perfectly together, as if they'd danced together a hundred times and not just a few minutes.

When he'd spun her around, their bodies had brushed against each other's. She was still reeling from the jolt of desire it had caused as his mouth had captured hers. His lips were firm, slightly covered in Jameson, and she'd lost herself in his kiss. He'd known everything she could have desired in a kiss – where to tangle his hands in her hair, how to subtly continue their dance on the floor, when to nip at her lower lip. She'd been practically panting with desire when he'd finally done it.

Asked her back to his place.

An alarm began to beep pulling her out of her still slightly drunk memories. Bridget looked up to see him stepping inside a ranch style home. Her body was still tingling, despite the twenty-minute ride out of Los Angeles to get to his house. She'd run her fingers up and down his arms the entire ride, and now she wanted to trace them along something else entirely different.

She stepped inside. His arms immediately wrapped around her waist and tugged her to him. The small silver clutch slid out of her fingers and dropped to the floor. Her body meshed against his, a perfect fit. They both made noises of approval as she rubbed against his jean-clad erection. His mouth seared a kiss across her lips, and moved to line a trail down her neck and stopped at the edge of the tube top part of her dress.

"I've been dying to take this metallic contraption off you all night."

Jeremy's voice was husky with desire and that mixed with his accent, made Bridget felt grow wetter. His teeth latched onto the elastic band at the top of the dress. He tugged it downward, using his hands to help as he went to push the fabric aside.

She'd gone without a bra, not liking the line it made in the tight dress and he growled. Bridget shivered as his hands came up quickly to cup her breasts in them. Her nipples pebbled at the contact, and she arched her body, thrusting her boobs into his warm hands.

"Just as I'd suspected, the perfect size."

He put his mouth onto her collarbone and slid his tongue against her flesh, just over the curve of it just before giving her a gentle nip. All the while, his hand's tweaked and tugged on her nipples. Desire clouded her thoughts for anything but the sexy southern man she'd met merely hours before.

Bridget shifted her hips. The dress dropped down further, exposing more of her body. She tugged off the garment, kicking it aside as she stepped towards Jeremy and pulled his head up to kiss him.

"You're wearing too many clothes for this, Jeremy," she whispered seductively as she stepped out of her heels.

He kissed her again, his tongue twirling inside her mouth and she moaned softly.

"We are also in the wrong room. I have this wonderful bed where we'll be going."

He didn't say another word as he swooped her up. A fire of need licked a flame through her. She held her breath as he made his way to the second door, nudging it open with his shoulder before walking them inside.

Jeremy was extremely controlled as he laid her down on the bed and let her go. Her eyes widened as he tugged the dark black button down off his shoulders. Bridget swore and licked her lips at the perfect way his shoulders looked and the circular tribal tattoo over his right pec.

She loved a man with a tribal tattoo.

Her eyes watched as he tugged off his pants. From her vantage point, she saw the way his erection tented his boxer briefs. Her whole body trembled at his size.

"One more second, Bridget."

She watched as he crossed over to the dresser and as she suspected, pulled out a condom. In the blink of an eye, he was back by her side, Jeremy lowered his body on top of hers just as she had blinked. The feel of his muscled flesh sent a shiver through her at the idea of such a powerful man just barely above her. He moved his hips and his erection brushed against her through her the small patch of thong that covered her.

He locked his eyes on hers. Bridget felt his thumbs slide under the white thong straps, tugging the flimsy underwear off her. His finger then trailed over her lips. She moaned and reached out to cup his erection in her hand.

"You're still wearing too much." Bridget grunted the last word out as he wrapped his tongue around her nipple and sucked it into his mouth.

She whimpered, and was barely able to tug his bottoms off as her body writhed under beneath his skilled mouth. Delicately, she wrapped a hand around him and couldn't help but notice the way her fingers didn't quite reach around his girth. "Wow."

He lifted his mouth off her breast and suckled on her earlobe. "I'll take that as a good thing." he grunted and shifted as she stroked up and down his length. "But nowhere near as good as that feels."

He shoved a hand between her legs. She cried out as he slipped a finger between her wet folds. He worked it in and out of her as his mouth covered hers. Bridget quickened her strokes on his dick and let go of him when his other hand covered hers. She squeezed her eyes close, eager to reach her climax. Her body cried out for his as he worked his finger back and forth within her.

Sliding his finger free, Jeremy positioned the tip of his cock at her entrance. She nodded at him and tugged his head down, deepening their kiss. Bridget felt every single inch of him as Jeremy sank deeper and deeper into her body. She felt herself tremble and her core walls tightening around him. She was needy and ready for her release. When he was finally seated all the way in she felt his kiss change and grow gentler before he pulled away.

"I want you to know, this isn't a habit of mine."

Bridget's lust began to ebb and grow hotter. She squirmed beneath him, trying to urge his body to move. Her laugh was strained at he gave her a lopsided smile.

"At this point, I don't think I'd mind either way, Jeremy."

To emphasize her point, she dug her fingers into his ass and pulled him into her as she wrapped her legs around his lower back and began to thrust her hips. No further words were needed as they lost each other to the moment between them. She felt every delicious stroke as his body thrust in and out of hers. Grunts and moans filled the room, though neither could distinguish whether the sounds were his or hers.

Their bodies slapped together and she felt the coils of her release tightening with every action. Bridget felt the passion building between them, getting ready to explode. His mouth found hers once more and their tongues entwined just as the damn broke, and she screamed her release into his kiss. Every second he continued, pleasure danced through her body. When his jerky thrusts quickened so fast she could hardly keep up she knew they were both nearing the end.

Bridget angled her hips, her breath catching as he dove deep within her. Jeremy grunted, the sound loud and long, before he carefully lowered himself onto her. The sound of contented pants rippled through the room.

She ran her hands up and down his back, relishing the way his muscles felt beneath her fingertips. They lay against one another for several minutes before he pulled himself away from her. His hand slid across her stomach as he gently tugged her to him. The subtle movement seemed a tad protective. For a moment, she forgot that this was nothing more than a wild night before she started her new life.

Jeremy slowly ran his fingers through her hair. Bridget smiled. She loved a man that wasn't afraid to cuddle after a round in bed and if he was even half as amazing as Jeremy was she was normally content.

"That was -" his voice trailed off.

"Mmm, it was."

She snuggled against him, enjoying the warmth of his body pressing against hers. Her eyes widened as he kissed the top of her head. The display on the digital clock read, three-thirty.

Shit.

The idea of going anywhere but to sleep next to her talented bed partner was unappealing. But she wouldn't start off on the wrong foot with the police department.

"Jeremy, I hate to say this, but I have to go. I start a new job this morning. That's why we were out tonight. We were celebrating."

She rolled out from under his arm and frowned at how cold she felt without him. Bridget didn't want this to be a reckless one-night stand.

He didn't say anything as she put her panties back on, though he did follow her downstairs. She slid back into the silver dress, toeing on her shoes and grabbing her purse. When she turned to look at him, the sight of anger and hurt lurking in his eyes pulled on her heartstrings. For reasons unknown to her, he was upset by the fact that she was leaving.

"Jeremy, I want you to know, I don't really do this sort of thing either. I mean, I have once or twice, when I've been extremely intoxicated after an industry party. But I don't do it as a habit."

The words rushed out of her mouth. A one-night stand shouldn't be anything more than a walk out the door. So why was she so intent on getting him to ask for her number?

Maybe it's the All-American good looks he has going. Or the way he pleased you like no one else ever has. Maybe you really did enjoy talking to him at the club, and it wasn't just your sex drive making you think you were.

She stood awkwardly before him, still taking in his prowess. He had removed the condom before

29

following her down. Bridget couldn't help but want to stay and see where how the rest of the night would keep going between them.

"Jeremy, I know this is extremely stupid. The look you have on your face indicates you enjoyed the time you spent with me, as I did you. I have a new job tomorrow, well today. I start training at nine am, and I can't be late. My father would kill me if he were alive, since I used his good name to get me the job."

She could see some of the anger dissipating as he unfolded his arms from across his chest. A small part of her couldn't help but feel flattered that he didn't like her screwing him and running out. She didn't even like that she was running out after the connection that was surging between them.

"I don't know why I'm being such a teenager about this." He ran a hand across the back of his neck. "I wasn't kidding when I said I don't do this. How about I agree with you, I liked spending time with you while we worked the alcohol off, and I certainly liked the time we spent together just now."

He flashed that side smirk grin of his and she clenched her teeth to avoid any rise of desire returning. She had to make sure she would leave and that damned smirk was lethal.

Jeremy reached for her bag. She let him take it, curious about what he was going to with it. A man digging in a woman's bag was not something that happened often, she admired his bravery. He dug within its depths and pulled her phone free. She cocked her head to the side and watched as he saved his phone number to the contact list.

"You say it's for a job. Sounds good enough for me. I put my work above everything else, so I can't fault you for wanting a good foot forward at a new one. So you can call me and we'll just have to figure out how to work backward – sex to dating."

He winked at her and passed the phone back to her. Her lips curved into a smile. She snorted.

"Problem. I didn't drive here. Care to give me a lift back home?"

Jeremy smirked at her. "Oh, and know where you live as well? Careful, Bridget. If I didn't know any better, I'd think you do want to date me."

His charm oozed out with every word he said. She closed the distance between them and gave him a quick peck on the lips.

"Keep thinking that line of thought, Jeremy."

She started to head out the door, her body thrumming with excitement. Not only would she be walking in her father's footsteps in a few hours, but because she might have also found the first man she'd ever been with who clearly didn't know she was a model and liked her anyway.

He chuckled and turned around. She heard him clomp up the stairs.

"Today is a new day, Bridget. Today, I'm going to start making you proud, Dad."

She smiled to the empty room, and waited for Jeremy to take her home.

2

Jeremy couldn't deny the thrum of satisfaction that was coursing through his body. It was already two o'clock in the afternoon and he couldn't stop thinking about Bridget. She'd been more than he'd bargained for. He was going to be sorely disappointed if she didn't actually call.

"Nice bust last night."

Jeremy looked up and nodded at the cop who'd spoken. "Thanks. It was about damned time."

The cop nodded and Jeremy kept walking. He hadn't been lying. Jeremy was a do everything by the books cop – no good cop, bad cop, no threatening the accused, and no trading for secrets with inmates. Which meant it took him almost three months to track down a drug cartel leader that operated between Los Angeles and Ventura and take them down.

"Way to go, Trellins!" another cop said, and smiled at Jeremy as he walked off the elevator and down the narrow carpeted hall to his desk.

"Jeremy, Captain wants to see you when you've got a second," Allendale, the only female cop currently on the drug rotation, informed him as he walked past her. "And good job, nice to know that scum is off the streets in full."

"Thanks. I'll get to him as soon as I can grab the work for the recruits."

Jeremy grinned and turned to the cubicle section in the center of the room. The grin on his face couldn't have been any wider.

He didn't do police work for the glory of it. But he certainly loved taking criminals down and had no problem accepting the praise of his fellow officers when he did.

His career always came first, which made picking Bridget up last night so rare. He didn't like women getting pissy about the fact that his job came first.

Too many relationships had gone south during the ten years since he'd joined the force.

He just assumed she'd be different. No real reason why, more like a gut instinct that told him she'd give him a shake. When she'd commented she needed to put work first, it had sealed the idea of asking her out in his mind. His pride still stung a bit that she'd been able to get under his skin, momentarily ruffling his pride.

Good sex can do that to a man. He laughed and dropped onto his desk chair to grab what he needed.

"Well, well, look at what the cat dragged in."

He heard Juarez taunt him as he sat down. Jeremy glanced at his buddy, and smirked at the older man. Juarez laughed and put his hand up for a high five.

"No, it wasn't like that. I mean, it was, but the girl I took home, she was a winner."

Jeremy grabbed a few files from his desk drawer and dropped them on the desk. He was in charge of a section of training and he'd need them to fill out the forms before they could get started.

"Well, how was it, then?"

Juarez laughed and another one of the guys who'd taken him out to celebrate the bust last night clapped him on the back.

"Yea, let's hear all about her, Trellins. I caught a glimpse of her and I'd have taken her home, too." Dominic chortled and sat on the corner of Jeremy's desk.

"Well, for my very first one-night stand, I'm excited to say that isn't a one-night stand. She said she'd call me tonight so we can plan a date." He smirked and snatched the paperwork into his hands as he stood up from the chair.

"You don't say?" Juarez chuckled.

"I do say. If you two don't lay off me about her, I'll be late, and the captain will have my ass tanned for it."

Jeremy walked away and he could hear the sarcastic comments continuing behind him. Truth be told, he didn't care.

He had enough to worry about. Getting saddled with another set of recruits wasn't his idea of a good time. After a chase last year that resulted in two totaled cop cars, he was stuck doing this for an unspecified period of time.

The only nice thing was it kept him from being assigned to any cases. So maybe he could ease Bridget into the idea of him being a cop, not immediately slam her into the lifestyle. He didn't relish the thought of rushing out at two in the morning to cover a homicide, or skipping anniversaries because he just couldn't stop running over the evidence till he found something.

Getting called in to speak to the captain rankled him. He avoided doing so whenever possible. "Maybe it's just a comment about yesterday, Jer. Don't get all worked up." He told himself just outside the office.

He rolled his shoulders and knocked on the wooden door. He saw the man gesture at him from behind the glass panels for him to enter and he pushed the door open and entered his superior's office.

"You wanted to see me, sir?"

Captain Danvers rose and extended a hand. Cautiously, Jeremy shook it back.

"Damn good job you did back there yesterday. Damn good."

The captain sat down once more. Jeremy couldn't help but feel elation at the praise. Danvers was in his early forties with graying temples and deep brown eyes, Danvers wasn't a harsh man. Though, he could be a hard-ass when the situation called for it. The only time he asked to see people was for three things—praise, scolding, and reassignment.

Jeremy sat down on the chair, but didn't lean back or get comfortable. "Thank you, sir. I'm disappointed it took so long to find them, but I'm happy as a clam to know we did."

Both men chuckled before Danvers spoke up. "I wanted to have a talk with you. A DEA agent was here earlier looking for you. Name of Malone. Have you been speaking with them?"

Jeremy swallowed hard. He'd never dream of going behind his superior's back to try to garner a position or promotion. The accusation made him nervous. He felt his Adam's apple bob back and forth as he swallowed once more as he looked at Danvers. The man didn't look angry.

"No, sir. I wouldn't do that."

"I didn't think so. Well, buck up. I'd hate to lose a detective to them, but it's more money than I'd tell anyone to pass up."

Danvers leaned forward, holding a business card between his index and middle finger. Jeremy never took his eyes off the man's but he did take the card. Working for a federal agency had been his dream, but he'd been screwed at Quantico when he broke his leg in the obstacle course. He'd decided being a cop would be just as good, and he hadn't wanted to risk his pride again.

"Now, get to those recruits. They could sure use some pointers from someone like you."

Danvers nodded and turned back to his computer screen. Jeremy got the message, stood up and left.

Today is a one of a kind day, isn't it?

He'd found a fun woman, gotten a little pride puff from his fellow officers and now had what sounded like a job offer from the freaking DEA. Although a part of him was pretty certain that Bridget was the best part.

He didn't want to admit it, but he craved having someone to share things with at night. Failed relationship after failed relationship had made him skeptical of such matters. Even of trying a relationship with her but he couldn't help but to want to spend more time with the sexy female that seemed to hide a wealth of intelligence and determination within her when she wasn't partying.

He'd gone up to Bridget on a whim. He never had problems getting girls when he tried, but she'd been so stunning that he'd watched her for almost twenty minutes. The way her body moved to the music mesmerized him and he had to have her.

When she'd broken away from the pack of abnormally attractive women she'd been with, he'd made his move. Sure, he'd only wanted a one-night stand, but there was nothing about that woman that he was ready to give up in one night. She was intelligent, sexy as hell and a firecracker in the sack.

Jeremy pushed open the door to the small makeshift classroom and froze in his tracks.

She was also standing right in front of him.

His mind spun out of control. His eyes traveled up and down her form so quickly he forgot to close the door as he took take another step inside. His eyes drifted over the way her black hair was tied back into a short little tail. The brown eyes he'd stared into last night as they had sex. Jeremy found himself admiring the small, but delicious curves of her body, that the outfit practically hid but he had memorized last night.

She wasn't breathing either. Her lips were parted and her eyes bore into his own, but she wasn't moving. This couldn't have happened. There just couldn't be a way she could be standing in front of him right now. Dressed in that uniform.

"Detective Trellins, everything alright?" Lieutenant Chase's question snapped him out of his shock just enough for him to move into the room.

"Sorry, yea."

Jeremy couldn't seem to take his eyes off her, and tried to convince himself that the woman couldn't be the same as the one he'd met the night before Because if she was, they certainly couldn't date. Jeremy dropped the paperwork down on the desk, and shook the confusion and dread he felt off.

"Good afternoon, recruits! I'm Detective Trellins. You'll be stuck with me every time you need a T crossed or an I dotted. So get used to seeing me, because I promise you'll hate me if you fuck your forms up." Jeremy barked out the order just as he did in every class he walked into.

Not only was he in charge of one of the learning segments, he was also the poor sap stuck with forms on the first day after they were briefed on how things would work and had a good lunch.

He couldn't help but notice the way Bridget sunk down into her seat. Jeremy wanted to frown; he much preferred the way her body had trembled when he'd spoken to her last night.

Shake it off, Trellins. Shake it off now.

"For the next hour, you're going to be filling out these forms. They're telling you everything from what time you wake up each morning to when the classroom and PT hours are. Do not scan them. Read them thoroughly."

Jeremy sat down in the second chair next to Stephen Chase, and watched as they all scrambled to orderly get up and grab the papers he'd set down.

When Bridget grabbed hers, their fingers touched. She gasped, but said nothing as she turned back to her seat.

Jeremy watched as they all filled out and read the forms. Day one had to be the most boring for a recruit. But he had a feeling Bridget wasn't feeling to bored right now. His brain didn't want to be in the same room with Bridget. It was too much of an aggravation for him to process, since he needed to say something to her.

"Times up." Jeremy heard Chase bark and they both stood to grab the forms.

He couldn't help but smirk at the few still scrambling to finish. There was no penalty. They weren't in some military boot camp, but he always liked instilling a little urgency in the new recruits.

"File outside and head to the lockers you were shown to earlier. Time for a little midday PT to see how much work you need." Nervous chatter erupted amongst some of the recruits as they rushed to their feet. "And Miss O'Casey, could you see me for a moment?"

What he was doing was ballsy, but they needed to talk now. He also needed to get someone else to help Chase with the first round of PT testing. Jeremy had a feeling that watching her sweat would wreak havoc on his libido.

He left the room before she did, but hung back as he waited for her to approach him. Jeremy knew he couldn't pull her over to a corner, which meant he'd have to control his volume and his expressions as they talked. All he wanted to do was a mix between shake her for not telling him and kiss her because of all the pent-up energy.

When she finally walked out of the room, she stopped so close to him that the toes of her boots touched his own dress shoes. Her eyes landed on his, though he couldn't make out what lurked in their depths. Neither of them spoke and Jeremy finally broke the silence by blowing out a breath.

"Why they hell didn't you tell me *this* was the job you had to be at in the morning?" His voice rose several octaves higher than he'd meant it to.

He lowered his head and moved his body in front of hers to try and block off some of their visibility. She was like a pixie compared to his tall frame.

"Excuse me, but why would I tell the man I'm randomly hooking up with during a one night stand where my career path is taking me?" her voice remained low, but it didn't lack any venom as she spat the words at him.

He flinched at the comment. Jeremy tried to not bring up the point that they were supposedly going to see each other again, and not at the precinct.

"That's not the point." He bit the words out and did his best not to back her into the wall.

"Yes, it is the point. You never said what your job was either."

He hadn't done so on purpose. "Because women tend to want to fuck me simply because of what I do for a career. and the others run screaming because I won't be able to treat them right with such a job."

Bridget didn't say a word. She blinked furiously fast but she didn't say anything.

"Nothing to say?"

"My father was a cop. I would've understood. I would have even said something to avoid a situation like this one." She gestured between them. "I really did want to see you later tonight." her tone was sullen, and he took a little comfort in knowing she was upset, too.

"Well, we're going to have to put that idea in the no pile. One thing you're going to learn about me while you train, I don't break rules. Ever."

Even when I want to, he thought.

"Well, it's not as if I'd want to jeopardize this. While being a model certainly offered a hefty paycheck, this is what I've always wanted to do, to be like my father. He's dead, in case you were wondering, so I *will not* ruin this."

She didn't wait for him to say anything else. It grated on his nerves that she thought she could just turn on her heel and walk away, which is exactly what she did.

That DEA job was looking better and better if that's what the offer really was, because he had a damned good feeling there was no way he and Bridget could pull off a side by side platonic relationship. Not if the erection he was sporting after just standing close to her was any indication.

She wasn't certain what to make of things as she stalked away from Jeremy. Thanks to her decade in modeling, she knew how to hold her shoulders and not stamp her feet like a child, but in her mind that's exactly what she was doing.

There wasn't a clear winner on what about the situation had pissed her off the most. The simple fact that he had to tell her to keep her mouth shut and that it couldn't happen again rankled her. He'd treated her as if she was some sort of a moron who didn't know any better. Or if what was pissing her off was the way she'd been dying to press her lips to his and tangle her hands in his hair while he'd been ranting at her.

"Wonderful. Your first one-night stand in almost eight years, and not only do you wind up wanting more than a one night stand, you pick a cop. A detective, no less." she muttered as she walked towards the lockers.

Bridget pulled open the door and hurried inside, not realizing how loud the booming metal door would be as it slammed into the frame. She cringed just as she reached her locker. The girl next to her laughed. Bridget turned, and must have been shooting daggers, because the other woman immediately apologized.

"Sorry. I've just never been able to resist laughing when people jump at a loud sound. I had a messed up childhood with some horror movies." The other girl offered her a hand, mirth shining in her light blue eyes. "I'm Ashley Pendle. Nice to meet you."

Bridget hadn't realized how badly she'd been looking for a friend today. She'd been hoping that someone wouldn't look at her and sneer the way

Ashley had done. She yanked open the locker and pulled out the regulation sweats.

"Bridget O'Casey."

"You're not related to Jimmy O'Casey, are you?"

Ashley's voice rose a little and was tinged with excitement. Bridget pulled herself back, unsure as to how someone could have known that.

"Um, yes."

She unbuttoned her uniform and pulled the short-sleeved shirt off. She'd already put on a sports bra that morning, so she tugged the dark blue cotton shirt over her head and tried not to grimace at how rough it felt. She should have bought them in advance and washed them first.

"My dad's Mark Pendle. They were partners–"

"- right out of the academy!" Bridget's own voice rose to match Ashley's excitement as she tugged off her shoes and pants, and slid into the workout gear.

"Exactly!"

"I didn't realize he had a daughter."

Her father hadn't spoken about Pendle since the man had moved away to Florida when she was a little girl. Bridget remembered some of the stories he'd told her, as well as the picture of him and Ashley's dad tacked to the wall in his office. Her mother would most likely never take it down.

"Stepdaughter, actually. He just retired. We've talked about this since I was in school. He wanted me to be a dispatcher. Which I was, for the last five years here, but it was time to go for broke and be on the other side of the helpful line. After about a year of begging, he helped me."

"Let's go, ladies. Time for chitchat can happen after class, if you aren't dead on your feet."

A female cop grinned down the locker room at them and all eight women in the room groaned, Bridget included. As they jogged out of the locker room to the indoor gym, she couldn't help but think about how interesting it was to be in the same class as her father's old partner's daughter. It almost kept her distracted from the way the men kept staring at her and gasping incredulously whenever she'd complete a set as instructed.

One thing was certain, even without the complication of Jeremy Trellins in her life, no one was going to make the academy easy for such a beautiful woman.

3

"This is never going to get any easier, is it?" Ashley groaned as she hit the unlock button on the key fob of her shiny yellow Jeep.

"Physically? God, it better."

Bridget agreed with every sore muscle and fiber of her being as she opened up the passenger door and flopped into the seat. Jeremy had been relentless in physical fitness today. What was worse, it had been a week, and he hadn't so much as looked at her.

A chuckle from the backseat made her turn and glare at Marcus Cochrin, a recruit that had been paired with them on a simulation last week. They'd bonded when they'd gotten the highest score.

"If you so much as say how it is for you, I swear I will run this car into the nearest pole just to make you hurt."

Ashley slipped a pair of sunglasses on her face and twisted the key into the ignition as she made the threat.

Bridget glanced at him through the rear-view mirror and smirked at him. They'd all become fast friends, carpooling and studying up after class when they weren't too dead to move. He was almost as good looking as Jeremy. Almost.

Jeremy would be like the night, all dark hair and sharp facial lines, but Marcus was light. He looked like a beach bum, whereas Jeremy held himself like a military officer. Marcus' hair was so blond that it appeared to be white, and it hung loosely at his shoulders now that the day was over. He'd been warned once that he was supposed to cut it. They were headed for the barber's. Lieutenant Chase threatened to have Marcus's hair shaved off if he didn't cut it. Somehow, they suspected that the lieutenant hadn't been screwing around when he'd said as much.

Marcus' skin was also deeply tanned from his days out on a fishing boat before he got tired of sea life and wanted to try something new. His face was the only clue that Marcus wasn't in his prime. Tight wrinkles played at the corners of his honey brown eyes that depicted an older man. To some extent, he was. He was thirty-seven years old, but he was proving that he could keep up with them every step of the way. Bridget wasn't entirely certain how he'd slipped past the age requirement, and when he'd been asked, Marcus had cracked a joke instead of answering.

"Aww, come on, Ashley, a guy's got to have some fun while being stuck with you two knockouts all day long."

He flashed a smile, his teeth gleaming white against his tanned skin. He chuckled as Ashley shook her head at him.

"Do you think you can take Mr. Smartass to get his hair cut? I want to grab something from the market since it's next door."

She needed to get an ace bandage, but she didn't want to tell them that. In the last week, she'd gotten the reputation of being a little Harpy based on how quickly she had taken some of the bigger guys down during defense training. Apparently, having a cop for a father hadn't impressed upon them enough that she wasn't pathetic. Grabbing the bandage would be like admitting she was just a slip of a woman and would undo all the work she'd done during the last week.

"Sure, I bet I can keep him looking handsome on his own."

They laughed at Ashley's statement and fell into an easy bickering pattern over what part was going to be the hardest during training.

"Look, I'm just saying, not all of us can be a toothpick and drop a man to the floor, Bridget. I'm going to have problems in defense training." Ashley commented as they pulled into the lot with a Great Clips and Vons. "I'm not saying the remembering shit won't suck, but you can force your brain to take on a lot more than you can force your body to be able to attack."

Marcus hopped out of the back of the Jeep. "She actually has a bit of a point. You're a beast out there, O'Casey. But not everyone can just magically do it. I, of course, will take you down in the next simulation for certain."

She snorted and closed the car door as she stepped out of it. "If you think so."

"Personally, I think she's waiting to take down Detective Trellins." Though Ashley's voice didn't hold a semblance of malice, Bridget stopped dead in her tracks.

"What makes you say that?" Marcus asked, beating her to the punch.

She remained frozen in place, unable to face them.

"Woman's intuition." Ashley laughed. "Have you seen the way they look at each other? Not that I can blame her. He's one of the hottest men I've ever seen. Add in his arrest record, and I'd jump him. Policy notwithstanding, of course."

Bridget blew out a deep breath, and still wasn't able to control her next comment. "You've heard the man all week in training. Don't break the rules or you're out on your ass. Even if I was looking at him like I wanted to sleep with him, it's not like it would matter."

Ashley's hand wrapped around Bridget's wrist and jerked her closer before she had a chance to move away. Bridget was spun around to face her friend's eyes.

"You did it already, didn't you?"

Bridget bit down hard on her lower lip. She hated liars. Absolutely hated them. If Ashley had noticed something between them, there was a good shot someone else had, as well.

So pick a side. Lie, or tell the truth. Trust your partners, or don't.

The last thought was her father's outlook on life. He'd always added in that not trusting your partner lead you both into a hell that was hard to climb out of. Her shoulders sagged as she let out a sigh.

"Not when you think we did." Bridget finally admitted out loud.

Ashley barely withheld a squeal and Bridget definitely heard Marcus cough behind her. "It was before training. Literally actually. Neither of us decided to disclose what we did for a living. The first time we found out was when he came in with those damned papers."

"Well, isn't that a story!" Marcus laughed. "Too damn bad that boy is as by the book as I've seen them. He sure as shit doesn't know what he's missing out on with you."

Bridget flushed at his words. She somehow knew the older man meant them. He may have been laid back, but she hadn't seen him be anything but brutally honest and assertive when he needed to be.

"It doesn't matter. We had a discussion that day, the first one, and it didn't happen as far as he is concerned. Neither of us can be reprimanded because I hadn't officially started and it won't happen again." She refused to acknowledge the bite of sadness she felt as she thought about things, especially since she'd clearly been visibly pining after him for a week. "So, let's just drop it."

"Fine, fine. But you may want to stop drooling every time he speaks in that sexy southern accent of his." Ashley laughed.

"Yea, easier said than done, but thanks for the warning."

"If you two are done being girls, can we run into Best Buy for a sec? I promised my brother I'd pick up a copy of the last Halo for him. I accidentally stole his, and then lost it overboard one night."

"Now that sounds very much like the Marcus I've come to know. Nothing at all like a cop." joked Ashley

"You just like me for my boyish charm, and the fact that when your shooting isn't enough, you'll know I can kick someone down."

They all laughed as they walked into the Best Buy. Like every other store she'd ever been to, it was a mass of colorful advertisements, bright blue shirts, and almost no customers. Her eyes skimmed over the displays from left to right —appliances, videos, cell phones and computers were scattered about. The back wall seemed to be composed of nothing but TVs.

Marcus took off in the direction of the TVs, and she caught sight of the video games to the right of where she stood.

"So, you really aren't going to do it again?" Ashley asked as they started walking towards Marcus.

"No, I'm really not going to do it again. He made it perfectly clear that we couldn't, and that I wasn't ever supposed to tell anyone. So we can't keep talking about it."

She was annoyed, more at herself for still wanting to talk to Jeremy than at Ashley for poking her nose in.

"I don't think there's any harm in a little bed play. It's not as if anyone would question your abilities physically, even after only a week. He wants you. I watch him watching you in training, and I'd bet anything everyone except stupid Marcus does. So just talk to him."

She shook her head. "The last time we spoke, I stalked off. He read me the riot act, he didn't ask me my opinion on the issue. I'm not here to find a guy anyway. I'm here to prove to myself that I can honor my father by following in his footsteps."

She crossed her arms and stopped at an end cap in front of the TVs, standing off to the side of the games aisle Marcus was casually strolling down.

"Breaking News - word of an attack on the Santa Barbra Police Department has just been confirmed. Three officers have been shot, and one is on his way to the emergency room. More information will be reported as we receive it."

Bridget's blood ran cold. Her eyes rose to the wall of TV's just as the blonde anchorwoman was replaced by a weather map. Her eyes darted from screen to screen as if one of the screens could possibly be a little bit behind the others. Unfortunately, they weren't.

"Did you . . . ?" Her throat felt dry and scratchy as she forced the words from her mouth.

"I couldn't have."

Bridget tilted her head and saw Ashley staring wide-eyed at the screens as well. Police stations were supposed to be safe. Despite everything that walked through the doors, it was supposed to be safe inside. Which meant that either a drive-by had occurred, or someone had walked inside and changed that fact.

"Do you think this will affect anything? I mean, if an officer, let alone three, has been attacked, they'll have to put everyone they can on it, won't they?" Ashley's voice sounded much like a little girl's, and Bridget was having trouble hearing her.

The phone call she'd received several months ago rushed back at her. The monotone voice on the other end–her mother's–telling her that her father had been shot, rang in her mind.

Bridget's breathing hitched in pace and she felt her body begin to tremble as fear and nausea raced a path through her entire body.

"Your father. Your father was shot, Bridget. I can't tell you anymore over the phone."

The resounding way her mother's voice had cracked on a sob was the same sound that tore past her lips as she stood in the middle of the store.

"Bridget? Bridget, are you ok?"

She couldn't process who was speaking to her as images of the police photos of her father, blood streaking down his chest, popped into her mind. Bile burned at the back of her throat. Bridget gagged, but forced it down.

Fingertips poked into her shoulders. Without thinking, she lashed her arms out, her fists in balls. Her balled fists connected with the soft flesh of a cheek, and Bridget heard the sound of a feminine cry at the same time as she felt someone grab her hands together.

Tears wet her face and she could feel how wet her cheeks were even as the images of her father and the sounds of her mother's sobs slowly started to fade. Bridget's eyes refocused and she looked down to see one of Marcus' large hands wrapped around hers. Ashley stood a bit back; her hand rubbing over her cheek.

A small crowd had gathered around them. Bridget's vision wavered slightly as the last of her tears trickled from the corners of her eyes. She blinked to clear them as she dropped her arms, showing Marcus that she no longer fought his sudden restraint.

"I'm sorry. I'm fine."

Heat licked a path up her cheeks, an indication of just how red the color blossoming against her pale skin would be. She didn't blush often, but there was no mistaking the sensation now. Marcus didn't release her hands. His honey brown eyes stared into hers, a mixture of sympathy and questioning shining in their depths.

"Are you certain?"

She took a deep breath and exhaled so slowly that she could feel every trickle of air leave her body. Bridget pursed her lips and she tried not to look at the crowd gathered around her.

"Yes. The news story brought unwanted memories. I'll be all right, though I'm wondering if we shouldn't forget everything and go study. Something tells me tomorrow will be a rough day."

Marcus's eyes never left hers as he slowly uncurled his fingers from around her hands. Once he let go, she reacted on instinct and pulled them down, rolling each wrist in a circle to feel for damage.

"We're going to talk about this on the way back," he said.

He walked away from her and made his way over to Ashley, who still hadn't looked Bridget in the eyes. The two started walking towards the front door.

Pain stung like a knife bite. Bridget pushed it back. She had only known these people for a week; she wasn't ready to tell them what had occurred with her father. However, She knew that after a display like this one, it was either share, or be on her own. She forced herself to take several deep breaths a few times, to try and force the news bulletin from her mind before she walked out of the store.

Bridget kept her head down once her feet finally began to move towards the door. Embarrassment was new to her. She hated the way she wished she had someone to walk out with like Ashley had. Someone named Jeremy with a scintillating southern accent and the smile of a football star.

She stopped as her feet touched the front tire of Ashley's Jeep. Bridget looked up to find the two of them staring at her.

"I'm sorry, Ashley. It was an accident."

Ashley nodded. Marcus spoke up, catching her by surprise.

"Rule 101, trust your partner. We're a team now and you need to let us in the loop. We have to know what we're dealing with to keep us all safe."

The comment was like a sucker punch to the gut. The air tore from her body again as very briefly, the image of her father being lowered into the ground flashed through her mind.

"You both know my father was a cop. One of the best beat cops there was. He'd had the shot to be more, but he'd always insisted on staying on the streets. It's because of him that I'm here. When I was growing up, he would tell me all the crazy stories and heroic moments. He was, without a doubt, my hero. We'd fought on more than one occasion about me joining up. Thirteen weeks ago, my mother called me. He was shot. No suspects. Just a handful of retired cops as witnesses, and nothing to go off on thirteen weeks later." She could hear her voice wavering as she put her hand on the door. "Can we just go? I'll answer anything you want in the car. I just don't want to be out on a sidewalk right now. It doesn't feel right."

Ashley opened the door. Marcus rubbed his hand up and down her arm before jumping in the back.

"I know you didn't mean it, but shit, let's make sure you hit the right people from now on. For being so boney, you have one hell of a right hook."

Some of the tension broke, and she was able to smile as Ashley pulled out of the parking spot. The fear and panic caused by the newscast hadn't disappeared completely, however.

"Marcus, did you hear it?"

Her eyes met his as she looked into the rear-view mirror and she watched as he swallowed hard.

"Kind of hard not to. And while we're talking about it, I don't blame your freak out, but you may want to get that under control. Cops get shot all the time. If you go into meltdown mode every time, your partner is going to wind up dead, too."

She gasped at the words, even if there was nothing but kindness in his tone, she would have sworn he had slapped her. But he wasn't wrong. In fact, he really couldn't be more right. She shut down in the store. Bridget knew she wouldn't be of any use if that kept up.

The silence grew thick around them, and the tension level amped back up. She pressed her head against the door and closed her eyes, trying to think of the one thing she knew that could make her forget about the news – Jeremy's hands on her body.

He could feel himself grinning like a fool. Trevor's body hummed with satisfaction as he kicked open the door to the hovel he had rented to store things. It was nothing more than a shack in Compton, but it did the trick. It had been a storage shack at one point for a little furniture store, but they'd gone under. He'd found the place during the time he'd spent locked up, and was paying in cash with the measly amount he made playing fast food cook.

This was a necessity. His parole officer could drop by for a chat or a search any damned time he wanted. So this was his private solace, his criminal outlet.

"Nothing will ever feel that good." Trevor said to himself gleefully

Glee filled his voice as he reached up and pulled on the string to turn on the dim light bulb. It buzzed in the silence of the afternoon; even Compton could be safe and quiet, at times. His eyes adjusted as the mid darkness gained faded to a dull yellow glow.

"Except the next time you do it."

He slung his backpack off his shoulder and let it drop to the dirt floor with a thunk. The gun probably should have been handled with better care, but aside from shooting them, Trevor didn't know much about guns.

"Until today, Trevor. Until today."

His grin spread over his face as another wave of satisfaction washed over. He dropped onto the tiny metal chair and let his eyes roll up the wall he'd spent the past five days setting up.

The back wall of the shack had a map of Southern California, one he'd bought from a bookstore with those giant atlases. He'd placed a giant red dot on every county name where the police had been involved in the arrest. The group he ran with had hit banks all over, so the cops been allowed to collaborate to bring them in was his guess.

Every county—San Diego, Santa Barbra, Santa Cruz, Ventura, and Los Angeles—had angry red dots on them. Plus a number written in black, one through six, indicating what order he would take them down.

He stretched his arms above his head and rolled his shoulders. The cracking of his bones made him sigh. Trevor stood up and grabbed the red marker. He put a giant "X" through Santa Barbara.

He'd hit the station there today.

Shooting the police had been a rush unlike any he'd ever experienced. Not even waving guns around to scare people while looting banks compared. His whole body had felt alive, on fire with excitement even. He couldn't even be certain as to how many he'd shot at.

He'd been in the parking garage about seven hundred feet away looking through a scope. Only when he'd fired the first round and hit a cop, had he gotten so giddy that he'd lost focus and took a few random shots. Staying and seeing what he'd done hadn't been an option. Thirty seconds after the shots were fired, he would have had cops all over his ass if he hadn't moved.

He'd calmly walked to the car and gotten in, zipping the gun inside the backpack before driving out. A few other cars had already been on the way down, some had stopped mid-drive, while others kept going. Trevor had forced his body to stop singing with excitement, and focused on keeping his eyes straight ahead.

He'd pulled out of the garage just in time to see the cops start chasing on foot after all the cars that had left. Trevor had bit his lip and sped off, unconcerned as to whether they'd seen him, since he'd removed the plates from the car and it wasn't his own. It now sat conveniently off to the side of the 101 with a popped tire. Someone from his old group had been waiting for him, just as they'd devised when they'd thought up the plan so long ago while he sat incarcerated for only part of a crime he committed.

Part of him had died sitting inside that cell. He'd answered to others, pretending to be fucking upstanding and moral, when all he'd wanted was some drugs and a way out. Now, he'd make part of the police force die. County by county

4

Bridget absentmindedly chewed on the tip of the number two pencil. It was a nasty habit from high school, but some how nibbling on the eraser calmed her down. They'd only been in the room for about eighteen minutes, and the chatter about the shooting around her was enough to send her into a meltdown. Ashley had placed her hand on Bridget's arm when the talking first began, but she'd shaken her friend off. While she was happy that the tension from the day before had washed out, she didn't need anyone questioning her. The less people that knew she was a cop's daughter, and that he'd been shot a few months ago, the better.

"Did you even think something like that was possible?" Jasper Candant, another recruit, asked the recruit to his left.

Bridget couldn't see whom he was talking to and she was too queasy to turn her head.

"I mean, right out of a parking garage, and then they randomly found the car on the 101. I wonder what they're going to say. I mean, this stuff happens," Margaret something-or-other said from behind Bridget.

"It's going to be ok. You heard the rest of the report. It was nothing like your dad's death." Ashley whispered the words, but the room was so loud, Bridget didn't think she had to.

Marcus pulled open the room door, strolling in with his hands in his pockets like he wasn't even late. His eyes landed on hers and she lowered her head. She and Ashley had spoken after they'd dropped him off, but she and Marcus had left things on a very strange note.

Hands appeared in her line of sight on her desk and she sighed as she pulled her head up. Marcus's honey brown eyes were softer than the day before. Bridget saw him cringe as another comment was brought up about what it's like to be shot as a cop.

"Hey, about yesterday–" he paused and took a deep breath. "I'm sorry. Not cool how I handled it. You're still young and losing a parent is about the most painful thing in the world. I meant what I said about needing to get your head around it, but how and when you do it is on your terms. Just make sure you let someone know when they're your partner."

She gave him a weak smile and he nodded. There wasn't time for them to say anything else on the matter as a stern voice cut through the room.

"That'll be enough of that." Captain Danver's stern voice boomed throughout the small room, and as directed, everyone shut up.

Marcus shuffled to the side and took the seat next to her like he had been doing since they'd met last week. She noticed Captain Danvers wasn't alone. Lieutenant Chase was with him, as well as a woman in a more business look. She certainly wasn't a detective, based on the lack of a holster or pockets for a badge. Her heels were also a good indication of that as well. The lead ball that had been sitting in her stomach all morning doubled in size and her nausea grew.

"I know you all want to talk about the incident yesterday. It would be impossible not to. However, being a police officer is a dangerous job. Your lives can and will be on the line more times than you'll hopefully be able to remember – because those aren't memories anyone needs to have."

Captain Danver's voice commanded the same respect it had when she'd heard him speak to her father on multiple occasions. He was younger then, but still just as impressive.

Murmurs rippled throughout the room. A well-timed eyebrow raise from the captain ceased the talking. They'd all met him last Monday, everyone knew he was the one in charge, and none were stupid enough to cross him.

"That being said, we do not talk about it. We do not aid in the spreading of rumors of what goes on amongst our own. If the media outlets approach you,

you decline. If you have a microphone shoved in your face, you politely take a step back. You do not discuss a police tragedy. You honor the fallen officers by letting them have their privacy. Myself, or another officer, will deal with the public."

Captain Danvers took a step back and nodded at Lieutenant Chase, giving him back his control over his recruits. The younger man nodded back and stepped forward, along with the polished brunette.

"This is Annalisse. She's the therapist here at the precinct and available to you should you need to talk. No one will think less of you for it. Mental stability amongst officers saves lives." The smaller woman stepped forward and gave a small wave and smile before lining back up with Chase. "We will be pushing forward. This is a tragedy, but stopping our lives for it won't help. Getting you ready to test and enter the force, that will. So, from this moment on, there's no more talking about it. No more whispers or notes passed like a bunch of high-schoolers. You want to talk, then you go to Annalisse."

Bridget watched as heads around the room nodded, and she felt hers nod as well.

"Very good. Lieutenant, take it as hard as ever today. Good luck to you all."

Captain Danvers and Annalisse walked out of the room. The door closed and it sounded a little louder than it had before in the abject silence.

A part of her wanted to scream with happiness that the topic was taboo. She wasn't ready to admit she needed Annalisse, not that she ever would. But Bridget would do what Marcus said if it was time to complete the course and she was still unstable. Her father wouldn't want it any other way. But for now, she was going to try and would handle this on her own.

Then there was the other half of her, the half that implicitly understood what it was like to lose someone to a shooting. She wondered just how hard it would be for everyone in the room to remain silent on the matter.

"Ok. Open up the packets we've been working on, and no one groan. You're adults," Chase's voice snapped at them.

For the past three days, they had been learning about police scanner codes. There were enough of them that even Bridget mixed a few up, despite her background in criminal studies.

Bridget wasn't mentally present and if they were going to have a test at the end of the unit, she knew she wasn't going to be able to pass this one. She'd removed the eraser from her mouth when the captain had begun speaking, and now casually slipped it back in between her teeth.

The entirety of the unit slipped by her as her mind pinged questions back and forth. Some that had no answers and others that simply didn't need to be asked. Bridget couldn't seem to force the questions to stop, and thinking about stopping only added to her lack of focus on the task at hand. Something else Marcus would probably yell at her for later on down the road.

How can they all literally just file it away like nothing happened? Because they've probably never had someone in their lives shot.

She answered her own question and felt a little foolish for even wondering. It was driving her crazy though, that everyone else really could just move onto the lesson like it was nothing. Maybe she really did need to speak to someone. She needed to get things under control before they got out of hand.

"Take a ten minute break. Grab some water. Detectives Trellins and Juarez will meet you at the shooting range in ten minutes. Stay in uniform. You don't ever shoot the gun without it on. While you may have been able to do so last week while we gaged where you were at, from here on out, until you pass the requirements, you'll only be doing so in the constricting uniform. It will be the thing that saves your life if you ever need to pull your weapon on a perp."

Bridget heard Chase, but she didn't move from her seat. She knew Marcus or Ashley might have noticed that she hadn't taken a single note. For that matter, she'd also bet that Lieutenant Chase had as well. The last thing she wanted was to be forced to go to Annalisse.

"Bathroom break?" Ashley's voice sounded far too cheerful.

Bridget wasn't interested in dealing with Ashley right now so she shook her head no.

She did however, get up and walk her friend out of the room.

"I decided I'm going to talk to Annalisse. If I can't push this from my mind on my own. Marcus was right. For as long as we're partnered during the courses, you deserve someone that won't drag you down."

Ashley laughed. "I don't think Miss Perfect Scorer could drag me down, but thank you. I appreciate it. I know it couldn't have been easy on you to come to that conclusion."

They walked to the range, with Ashley peppering her with police codes. She barely noticed Jeremy when they pushed the gate open. Her eyes lingered on his form, but she didn't hesitate or mention him to

Ashley as they grabbed their weapons, put the noise-cancelling headphones and goggles on.

Too bad it didn't last once Jeremy started to talk. His voice slid over every inch of her body. There was no sensual slide of his southern accent as he explained the score they would need to aim for today. However, she was so intently focused on the pout of his lips that everything he said didn't match the words she was hearing.

In her mind, he was telling her that they were going to make it work. That they'd be secretive. Careful, even. She sighed as the fantasy Jeremy leaned down and placed his lips to hers, sending a jolt of need through her.

Ashley looked at her sideways. It was only then that Bridget realized Jeremy wasn't in front of them anymore. A pop sounded next to her, indicating that they'd been given the all clear to start as well.

"Something tells me that look has absolutely nothing to do with the shooting."

Ashley winked and stepped up to the line on the floor, aiming her gun at the black drawing of a man's body.

"Just shoot your damned gun, Ashley."

There was no anger in her voice, just a playfulness. It was nice having a friend she could talk to about anything. It was something she hadn't had in ages because models had a nasty habit of spreading things they were told.

Ashley probably couldn't hear her, but she fired her weapon anyway. The bullet slammed squarely into the target's shoulder. She fired off six more rounds, not targeting the man's chest, or the proper place of the head to obtain the needed points. Her shoulders were slumped a little as she turned and walked over, giving Bridget the space she needed to take her own shots.

"Don't focus on it, Ashley. We can rent guns at shooting ranges anytime you want."

Bridget had to shout to get over the sound of shots going off at different intervals, and she watched as several heads turned towards them. Ashley's cheeks flamed red.

"Sorry," she mouthed to her friend.

Bridget turned and let out a deep breath as she focused on the fresh target that one of the other cops in the room had switched out so she could do her own practice.

Letting out the breath she'd taken she depressed the trigger. The first bullet shot from the barrel and slammed into the center of the drawing's forehead. A flicker of excitement went through her. She'd gone shooting more than once as a child with her dad, but using the skills she'd learned right now held a great deal of satisfaction for her.

I wonder if Jeremy has ever questioned how I'm able to do this.

The stray thought slipped into her mind as she took the second shot. It was a little high on the left shoulder, but close enough to the heart to get the point level she'd wanted.

Pausing just for a second she chastised herself for thinking about Jeremy. There was no room for thinking about a man anymore than there was room for thinking about the shooting from yesterday. She needed to clear her mind and do whatever it took to not think about the positively sexy dimples every time he smiled or the way she'd wanted to run her fingers over the fresh buzz cut he had.

She closed her eyes and fought off the mental picture even as desire bloomed within her. Her breathing slowed. Bridget forced breath after breath. It felt like an eternity passed before the images left her alone. Without flinching, she opened her eyes and fired off the seven allowed shots. Every one of them landed so close to the initial shoulder shot the holes touched. Except for the one she'd expertly shot through the center of the target's right hand.

Bridget tried not to beam at anyone, especially Jeremy when her eyes caught his as she turned around. She quietly went to stand next to Ashley at the back of the shooting line to indicate they were done and ready to be scored on the practice shots. Over the next few minutes, the outpouring of gunshots grew quieter and her anticipation over learning the results grew stronger.

If she'd succeeded in accumulating enough points while stressed and indulging in a fantasy about the officer in charge, then she wouldn't need Annalisse. She just needed a little time to decompress. Learning the material wasn't a problem. She may have been a model and a college dropout, but she wasn't a moron. She could learn and memorize with the best of them. Granted, her stature put her at a disadvantage for the physical tests. She'd struggled through the PT sessions enough to know she needed everything else to be perfect.

Her fingers tapped on the wall she was leaning against as the time ticked by. No one spoke as the targets were all removed. They could have left, could have gone out of the range and taken a breather before whatever was coming next. No one seemed inclined to do so, however. With the threat of police shootings hanging over their heads, she guessed every one of them wanted to prove accurate with a gun. Their lives all could depend on it one day.

She couldn't help but watch the muscles in Jeremy's back flex. He stood to the left of her, about a hundred yards away, tallying up the scores, while the man he'd introduced as his partner, Juarez, did the same with the other half. The muscles in his neck corded as he counted silently, moving his lips as he did so. She licked her lips as an image of their having sex flashed through her mind.

Bridget shifted her body weight and downcast her eyes.

The fantasies angered her, she had no control over them and she was putting her career in jeopardy every time her mind wandered. For all intents and purposes, Jeremy had seemed to be the one with some investment in taking things further. His display of annoyance when she wouldn't stay the whole night the night they'd slept together had seemed indication enough but maybe she was wrong.

No one would ever know that based on his behavior now. He was completely cut off from her. In fact, unless it was to bark an order at the unit as a whole, he hadn't said a word to her since last

Monday. His eyes met hers on many occasions, but there was no sign of anything akin to longing in them. In fact, he typically narrowed his eyes at her and pursed his lips before crossing his muscular arms over his chest and turning away. Nor was there a single indication he'd so much as cared that the attempt at a relationship they'd been interested in a week ago was extinguished.

"If you hear your name, you've qualified. There will be no stress in any upcoming sessions. However, you will be mandated to come often to the shooting range and practice. The next assessment will involve moving targets. Anyone that cannot complete the stationary one in the required time will be spoken to and possibly dismissed if deemed appropriate," Juarez said.

She flinched a little, even knowing that she'd shot perfectly, nevermind perfectly enough to get the score she needed. It didn't mean she wasn't concerned about Ashley and Marcus though.

"Congratulations, Miss O'Casey–highest score. I see your father left you with something after all."

Juarez smiled at her and she flushed, hating the fact that her secret was now out. "Tolbert, Voll, Ramakers, Spano, Honeysett, and Finnin. Congratulations, and consider helping your fellow recruits with tips."

Bridget smiled over at Marcus, pleased by the fact that he had passed, but did her best not to look over at Ashley. Being the daughter of a cop, she most likely wasn't content with the knowledge she hadn't passed her first try. Bridget knew she certainly wouldn't be if they were in opposite positions.

It just meant she'd have to try and help her partner in any way she could. Besides, she needed a little girl talk. Maybe another night out to take her mind off the sexy detective who clearly wanted nothing to do with her.

It had only been one night. The fact that she saw him daily was the only reason her body kept craving him. At least she hoped that was all because she had a strong feeling she'd more than enjoyed their conversation before they'd wound up racing down the streets to his house that night.

Jeremy rubbed a hand over his eyes and gave Juarez the one finger salute. "Just don't get cocky. I knew splitting the recruits in half would give you something to brag about." He laughed as he pushed open the glass door leading to the garage.

"Look, pal, it's not my fault your half have no natural talent."

"It's not natural talent. Your lead scorer was a cop's kid." he muttered, feeling bitter about that fact.

Bridget O'Casey had left a whole hell of a lot out of the "hi, how are you's" they'd done that night. Starting with the fact that her father was one of the most respected beat cops ever to come out of the LAPD because of his dedication to the beat. The man had worked twenty-one years as a beat cop, with an occasional stint in Vice. He had wanted to remain close to quick crime and leave the long winded victories to the men and women with more patience.

Juarez chuckled and pulled open the door of his beat-up blue 1980's Mercedes. "Like I said, not my fault. Maybe you'll do better next assessment." He dropped into the driver's seat and grabbed the door handle, but didn't pull it closed. "Ya know, I almost don't mind that you've dragged me into your punishment."

His partner smirked and pulled the door shut and Jeremy walked off.

He'd been out of sorts since learning Bridget was a recruit, and had gone to Juarez for help. The only explanation had been that he was mentally drained from the recent bust and needed help. The truth was, he didn't trust himself with coming into such close contact with Bridget on a frequent basis.

For the past three nights in a row, he'd dreamt about her lithe body thrusting beneath his as they frantically reached a climax. Twice, he'd dreamed they were on simple dates, a day at the beach and a night at the movies. None of which had made his morning moods pleasant.

He knew how she felt about him by the way she looked at him. The way her eyes would widen and her mouth would part on a small gasp when he would look in her direction. Lust rode him hard every damned time. He had no clue as to where the strength to ignore her came from.

Bridget O'Casey wasn't a woman any man could easily be able to ignore. Toss her long legs, perfectly sculpted face and perky breasts aside, and she was still a force to be reckoned with. Her father had taught her well. She was the best shot in the class. He knew it had nothing to do with impressing him.

Jeremy had watched her during the three days they'd been training. She kept her focus at all times. She suffered a little in physical training and it pained him. She held onto the standards, but she didn't complete the tasks with the finesse or speed she used while completing the mental tasks and shooting. They hadn't begun any self-defense training yet either. For that, he was grateful. The idea of watching her body beneath any man's but his own wasn't on his to-do list right now.

The idea of sparring with her, of pinning her to the mat and lowering his body weight on top of hers so she could squirm and force her way out made him groan as his hand wrapped around his car's door handle. He could feel the rush of blood to his dick and if he didn't find some other way to forget about Bridget, the remainder of training was going to be impossible on them both. He had a feeling they could only avoid each other for so long before things grew a little more cumbersome between them.

It wasn't until he was pulling open the door that he looked up and around his own car. A frown marred his face and he sucked in a breath. Bridget and her partner, Ashley, were standing next to a yellow Jeep two cars down.

"Fuck." He jerked the car door open, and tried to get in and get out of the way, but he heard his name before he had a the chance to do so.

"Hi, Detective Trellins. Wonderful afternoon!" Ashley waived at him as she got into her car as Bridget was walking towards him.

He stood up from the car seat, standing in between the seat and the door, waiting as she walked up. The sway of her hips in the blue leggings wasn't covered enough by the dark burgundy tunic she wore. He felt that tiny spark of lust flare within him at the sight and he bit down on the inside of his cheek, trying to not make a sound.

"Detective Trellins, do you have a moment?" Bridget's voice sounded sweet, and there was no indication of the ire that shown out of her eyes.

"Not here."

He ground out the words through clenched teeth. Bridget didn't move away. Instead, she took half a step closer to him. Jeremy felt his dick pulse within his pants.

"I'm not going to be loud or even say anything that can incriminate Mr. Perfect in a night of passion with his subordinate."

True to her word, she lowered her voice. The problem was the sultry tone of it made his heart beat quicker.

"What I'm going to do is tell you that we're both adults. That we slept together before we knew anything, and we broke off any possible shot at doing it again once we found out the problem."

He was breathing heavily, trying to resist the urge to pull her face down to his. "So what's the point of this quiet little tirade then?"

She stepped closer, leaving just enough space between them that it couldn't be considered completely inappropriate. Bridget grazed her stomach across his pelvic area, and he growled low.

"The point is, you were not an adult when you approached me about it and I would like an apology."

The glint in her eye told him there was so much more she wanted. He was losing any ability to resist her with every second they stood out there and sooner or later, someone else was going to walk out of the precinct. He could only hope she walked back to her friend before that happened.

"Get. In. The. Car." He forced the words out and heard his own deep ragged breaths that followed his command.

Her response was a slow and subtle grin that sent another pulse of heat to course through him. She didn't waste any time as she walked around the car and pulled the door open.

He watched as Ashley started to get out of her Jeep, a look on worry plastered on her face. Not that he blamed her, she had no idea what Bridget and he had done. Getting into the car with your sort of teacher was stupid.

"We're going to talk about the shooting range," Bridget said as she gazed at Ashley. "I'll find another way home."

The statement sounded ludicrous. Jeremy had a feeling she knew that and it was intended to get an eyebrow raise from anyone that overheard. She wasn't going to implicate him directly, but she was willing to play dangerous games. That shouldn't have aroused him, but it did.

He slid into the driver's seat and gripped the wheel so tightly that his knuckles turned white. His gaze dropped to her hands, watching as she clipped the seatbelt in place. It was the most non-sexual thing he had probably ever had turn him on.

When she turned to look at him as he was pulling out of the garage, he couldn't resist the pull to look at her. The desire in her eyes matched what he was feeling, and the way she was chewing on her lower lip was driving him mad.

"Is this what you wanted, Bridget? An adult action like this one?" his lips captured hers almost before he finished speaking and the kiss was over as quickly as it had begun.

She slid her hand into his lap, just shy of where his cock pulsed with need, and let it rest on his knee. "I think this is what we both want. Getting it out of the way will make it so much easier on us both."

"Don't count on it, Darlin'."

Jeremy pushed the words out and cranked up the music, it was afternoon but he was still a good thirty minutes from his house. If she kept playing him like this, they weren't going to make it.

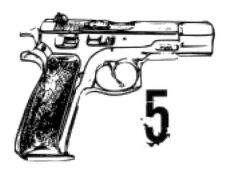

5

We've been here before.

The thought rolled through Jeremy's mind, and he forced a deep breath out through his nose. This would make it the second time that lust and chemistry had sent the two of them barreling towards his house in his little car.

"Are you certain about this?" Bridget's voice held all the lust it had before, but also twinge of concern laced her words.

He pulled open the door and grabbed her hand to tug her inside, kicking the door closed behind him. "There is no part of me that thinks this is a good idea." His voice was gruff. "However, men tend to not think with their brains in situations like this."

He closed the distance between them then, and wrapped her in his arms and placed his lips on hers. Her reaction was instantaneous. She wrapped her arms around his neck, molding her body wonderfully against his own. His lips moved gently across hers, the kiss was shallow but sparks still danced across his senses coming alive.

As she ran the small tip of her tongue over the seem of his lips Jeremy groaned with need and she slipped her tongue inside his mouth. Jeremy's hands gripped her waist harder as their mouths brushed together and their tongues swirled about, tasting and learning what the other liked, more so than they already knew. His whole body ignited with need the more aggressive her kiss became. Bridget wasn't a shy and gentle flower, he'd already known that, but feeling her lust take control of the situation was a turn on he hadn't ever imagined.

Bridget's hands dropped from around his neck. She ran both down the front of his perfectly ironed white shirt. She gently tugged on the tie as she nipped at his lower lip. He let go of her waist and slid one hand into her hair to pull her head down further. The other found the waistband of the leggings she'd put on after they'd been released. With one swift motion, he'd pulled them down. He leaned back from the kiss to press a trail down her neck and nipped at her collarbone.

Her hands were not done. She made quick work of the buttons on his shirt while small pants slid past her lips. Her breaths were deep as his hands massaged her breasts through the tunic she wore. Her fingers were warm and feather light as she shoved the now open shirt off his body. To facilitate, he removed his hands from her and took a moment to pull her top off. Desire shone in her eyes as she looked over his chest.

"Like what you see?"

She didn't flush and even dared to raise her electrifying gaze to his. "More than you know."

She stepped towards him before he could even take in how nice her breasts looked in the boring white bra she wore. Bridget pressed a kiss to his left pec and then his right before her tongue trailed a path downward, outlining his abs. His body shivered at her touch, his dick throbbed hard within his pants. He didn't know how much longer he was going to last.

When her lips brushed against the lowest part of his stomach his hips bucked and he growled as he buried his hands in her hair. Bridget's hands were quick, she wasted no time in jerking the zipper down on his navy pants. Looking deep into his eyes, she pulled on them just once before tugging both his pants and boxers off at the same time. She moaned as she reached out and gently grazed her fingers across his shaft. He felt her spread the few drops of liquid that had seeped out of him across the tip of his cock.

"I hadn't realized exactly how much I've wanted to do this until now." she said the words playfully

Bridget knelt before him and ran her tongue down the length of his shaft before making her way back up. His hips bucked instinctively towards her. She chuckled; a low throaty laugh and it wreaked even more havoc on his libido.

She said nothing else as her mouth closed over the head of his cock, taking in nothing more than that little part of him. Her cheeks hollowed and she sucked hard on his tip as her tongue swirled over it. She was driving him mad and she had hardly done anything.

"Bridget." His hips rolled in circles before her, and his hands remained locked within her hair, urging her to take him completely.

There was no warning as she opened her mouth and pulled back. Cool air raced over his wet cock. She took him in her hand and stroked him from base to tip a few times. Bridget lightly used her fingertips and cupped his balls to massage him just before she took him fully in her mouth again.

Stars flashed across his vision and he almost came in her mouth on the first stroke. She knew exactly how to move, what pace to take, and how badly he liked a woman taking him to the hilt in her mouth. When her strokes sped up, he realized how frantically his hips were thrusting his cock into her mouth in time with her own bobbing sucks.

It took every ounce of willpower he had to say her name. "Bridget, if you don't stop, I'm not going to make it to the really good stuff." He could feel how tight his muscles were stretched, his release was hardly a few strokes of her tongue away.

When she pulled back he blew out the breath he had been holding. Bridget stood and pressed her lips against his. His entire body shook with desire, and when she pulled back he wondered if she was as dizzy with need as he was.

"We can't have that now, can we?" She gave him a saucy smile and it unhinged the last ounce of restraint he had.

His hands went to her underwear and jerked the solid white boy shorts off so quickly that he caused her to stumble a little. He felt guilty, but loved the way her breasts pressed against his chest when she did.

In a swift motion he lifted her in his arms and walked towards the couch. He sat down, spreading his legs a little apart, shifting her around so that she could straddle his body. He could feel how wet she was and he couldn't resist swiping a finger over her folds to see just how wet.

Jeremy wasn't sure who moved first, but he felt her hand wrap around his shaft and place him against her entrance. He bucked his hips and slid inside. They both made a noise of appreciation and he wasn't sure who enjoyed the motion more. Bridget wiggled her hips and leaned back ever so slightly, taking his whole length into her body.

She bent her head lowered and kissed him. He slid his hands across her hips and began to rock against her body. Bridget didn't need any encouragement and began to ride him. Every time her body sank down onto his cock, he wanted to hold her still and enjoy the feeling of being wrapped inside of her. Bridget refused to let him hold her still for long though, and continued to slide all the way back up his length and sink down just as quickly.

His mouth moved against hers, the kiss rapidly speeding up to match the thrusts of their bodies. The sounds of their arousal and enjoyment were the only noises in the living room.

His head spun and he couldn't form any thoughts. He was lost in the sensations coursing through his body as their bodies moved together.

His release caught him off guard, barreling through him like a sudden storm, and he groaned her name into their kiss. He continued to thrust himself into her before he broke the kiss. Her eyes opened and she held his gaze. He watched and grew excited as her eyes slowly lidded over and her mouth parted on a half shout as her body came around him.

She continued to ride him as her walls milked his shaft. He shuddered, loving the way she felt against him. They continued to move together slowly, just feeling each other for a few more minutes until she finally stopped. Jeremy unlatched his fingers from her hips and Bridget laid her head against the curve of his shoulder; her hot breath sliding across his flesh.

"Wow." she panted.

He tried to form a coherent thought, but just nodded instead before he was able to talk. "Maybe all that waiting had a benefit after all."

"Mmm, maybe not." she said as her fingers swirled over his shoulder and down his back. It tickled a little and he twitched at the sensation. "There is no possible way that could have been any more perfect."

"Bridget–"

His voice held a cautionary tone. Jeremy wished his mind hadn't already flipped to the next thought.

"I know what you're going to say next, Jeremy. I have no idea how you plan to pull it off, because if this is what sex is like twice, there is no way I'm going to willingly give you up. I want to know you. I want to be with the sexy, tough as nails detective whose southern accent can melt my panties right off me and look like he's stepped out of a photo shoot."

"There may be a way." The words were out of his mouth before he realized what he had said.

She looked at him, curiosity spreading across her beautiful features. "Go on, Detective."

"I was offered a job at the DEA last week. It's an opportunity most cops would kill for." She remained quiet, waiting for him to continue. "But I like who I am at the station. I like my partner. I like doing what I do."

She frowned, and he felt a little guilty.

"Jeremy, don't change your lifestyle for some hot sex. As much as I want this to continue, we have no idea what we have. Unless you count the really hot sex and the basis of the one conversation we had together. Relationships are certainly created on less, but not life changes."

She didn't realize how much her words meant to him. No woman had ever understood why he loved his job so much. Yet here he had one that was sexy, smart, and a damned good recruit. Unfortunately, he wasn't able to do a thing about it.

"I can't tell you how much that means to me. Women aren't always the most accepting of this career and I can think of a million who would've leapt at the chance to tell me to go work somewhere else if it meant our relationship could work."

She gave him a coy smile. "Well, let's just say I know a thing or two about taking jobs that I don't really want to please others."

He hadn't realized she hadn't loved modeling. The knowledge itself brought them a little closer. They were more and more alike each time they spoke no matter how brief the conversation.

"But I haven't completely decided against it. The pay raise alone is hard to walk away from. I just don't know if I want to do drug busts full-time. I like the other cases, and the others I help as well."

A comfortable silence settled over them. She gently slid off his body and moved to sit next to him on the couch. He loved the way she could be so dainty, yet so aggressive at the same time.

"So we mark this off as taboo and try not to find ourselves here again? Act like adults and not interact?"

"Somehow I don't think either of us can do that. Not that it's horrible that we can't. I like you, Bridget – a lot. I don't care how long or short we've known each other. I've watched you these past few weeks and I can see who you are. It's someone I don't want to be kept away from."

She kissed him then, a. quick peck and it made a smile form on his on face.

"Go on, I rather like what you're saying."

"Let me talk it over with Chase, you won't believe this, but I'm on training classes because I did fuck up last year. I got a lot of damages charged to the department trying to chase down a drug dealer. The teaching has been my penance. In the mean time, do you think we could just, I don't know, lay low with it?"

Bridget chewed on her lower lip in thought. Her black hair tumbled into her eyes as she looked down. He didn't think about the intimacy of his own gesture as he reached over and traced his fingertips over her cheek, tucking the strand behind her ear.

"I think we can do that. On the condition that we spend the night together. I'm not ready to go back to pretending I don't have the world's hottest crush on my teacher just yet."

She winked and they both laughed.

"I absolutely can't find a single thing to argue about that, Darlin'."

***

Jeremy's mind raced with excitement, his nerves on edge. He'd barely gotten to the precinct early after dropping Bridget off. He had about fifteen minutes to catch Chase before he headed to the basement level and the classroom. Today they would start the unit on sparring, which meant there was no way in Hell he could be there with Bridget present. Not when his body had a solid memory of what it felt like to have hers squirming and thrusting beneath and on top of his.

He took a deep breath. If there was one person he could trust with his secret, it would be Chase. They'd been good partners prior to Chase getting to move up in ranks. They'd shared more than a partner's fair share of drinks, and had certainly talked about sleeping with women and personal issues. That didn't make this any easier.

Jeremy lifted his left hand and rapped his knuckles across the door to Chase's office. The sound echoed off the thick wood door. He soon heard a muffled response telling him to come in. Slowly, Jeremy pushed the door open and walked in. Chase looked every bit the important police officer. His desk was cluttered with an unending stack of paper. Two monitors sat on his desk and he appeared to be glued to both of them.

"Hey, partner, you got a second?"

Jeremy sat down in the chair opposite Chase. His heart pounded within his chest, and he wondered if this was the right way to go.

Chase looked up and grinned. "Hey there, partner. Wow, seeing you in classes wasn't enough? Got to stop by the office now? What do you need? I've only got about ten minutes."

"I've got to talk to you about something, well, someone really."

Chase pulled his hand off the mouse and looked up at him. "Oh, really? Maybe it's the woman you disappeared with last week from the club? Still dying to hear about her, you know."

He laughed, and for a second, Jeremy forgot about the severity behind his visit. "I'll say this. She was as hot in bed as she was out. Best decision I've ever made."

Chase smirked and put his hand up for a high five, which Jeremy awkwardly returned. "So, you just came to talk about a hot night in bed, almost two weeks later?"

Jeremy cringed and ran a hand over the back of his neck. "Well, I suppose it is about her. But it's really about a recruit."

"Shit."

Chase offered him nothing more, and Jeremy sighed.

"Pretty much. I've slept with a recruit. It was that night. She was at the club and neither of us volunteered any information to the other about our personal lives, not career wise at least."

Chase swiped his hands across his eyes, slowly drawing them down, giving him a very ghoulish effect. "Let me take a guess, O'Casey?"

Jeremy nodded, not shocked that he hadn't pulled one over on Chase. "That easy to tell?"

"She's hot and a damn good recruit I've seen the

way you look at her. I just assumed you were fantasizing about getting a piece of ass, not that you'd already had it."

Jeremy sucked in air through his nose and exhaled loudly. "It was just that one time. I'd essentially accosted her when I saw her last Monday. I hadn't gone near her since and it was why I'd roped Juarez into helping."

"Good, then just keep distancing yourself. Don't think twice on it. Mistakes happen, and she wasn't a recruit then."

"That's the problem. Apparently being a brute didn't go over too well with her. She cornered me yesterday in the parking lot. Before I knew, it we were back at my house."

"Fuck. Do you realize what this could do to your career? To hers? She's damn good and getting into bed with you will fuck you both over. It has to stop. I don't care what you do to make it happen, but it does need to happen. I won't see you throw everything away for a piece of hot ass. I can't believe we've seen the day when by the books, Jeremy Trellins, throws it all away for a woman."

He ignored the jab at his track record and pushed the conversation forward. "Precisely why I'm here. Well, partially. I want you to talk to Captain. Tell him that I don't belong in the room with her. Just leave out that it's happened again."

He wrung his hands together, waiting for Chase to ask the next question.

"You're not seriously considering not ending it? Trellins, tell me that's not the look I see in your southern boy eyes right this minute."

"I'd be lying, Stephen."

"Son of bitch, you even used my first name. Is she worth it, Trellins? She worth the career of a lifetime, the respect of your family?"

Chase asked the question he'd been afraid to answer before. He and Bridget had decidedly ignored the topic last night. Rightfully so, as all they had was incredible sex and strong chemistry. He knew the answer, however, and it slammed into him like a force to be reckoned with. He wasn't ashamed when he looked at Chase.

114

"Absolutely. Sure, she's hot and fantastic in bed. Bridget O'Casey is a hell of a lot more than that. I've watched her in training. She's intelligent, strong, funny, a good potential cop, and someone I can't seem to stop wanting to be around. Yea, she's worth the potential fuck up. I may be saying that because the DEA came around two weeks ago. They offered me a job starting the first of the year, if I want it."

Chase let out a low whistle, but said nothing for a few seconds. "Damn, why didn't you start with news like that? Congrats, Jeremy. Seriously, that's some of the best damn news I've heard in awhile."

Jeremy didn't have time to preen over his friend's well wishes. "I'm not certain I want to take it. I like what I'm doing here. Juarez is a damned good partner. I don't know if I want an entire life dedicated to undercover ops, drug busts and high payout crimes like that. Sometimes, it's nice just to grab a burglar, ya know?"

Chase shook his head. "No. No, I can't say I do. That might be why I'm sitting behind this desk job and you're out blowing up cop cars." The comment was good-natured. Jeremy let out a breath he hadn't realized he'd been holding. "But why not take it? It would solve a lot of problems. If you're really wanting more with O'Casey, it would open the doorway just fine."

"That's just it. I don't want to take it simply because it would allow me to have a relationship." He sighed almost whimsically. "It would be nice, though, to be with a woman who won't freak out when I get a call at one in the morning. Or bitch that I'm not home for dinner when I'm a hairsbreadth away from catching a murdering scumbag."

Chase stood up and walked out from behind the desk and clapped him on the back.

"I understand all that, but then you've gotta put whatever you have with O'Casey on ice. You've got a back-up plan if you're caught? Does she?"

Jeremy processed the words and frowned. Chase was right. He had another job he could run to if he damned his place with the LAPD. Bridget only had a modeling career, one she didn't like. Which meant they couldn't see each other, not until he made a choice about the DEA.

"We talked about cooling it off for awhile. But if I keep seeing her everyday, or even every few days, it's not going to help. So I need to you talk to Captain. Think of all the scraps I saved your ass from in the past. Consider this me calling in an old debt."

"Damn it, Trellins. Fine, I'll talk to him now, but you better promise me you won't get in any deeper with this girl. It won't help anyone if you do. If I let the captain know I knew anything and didn't share it all, it could blow up on me, too."

"Deal."

Chase walked out of the office, grumbling something that Jeremy couldn't actually hear properly enough to understand. He flinched as the heavy door slammed closed behind his friend, leaving him alone in Chase's office in the silence of his admission.

Jeremy kept turning the conversation over and over in his mind. He didn't want to take the DEA offer simply because it would allow him a relationship. Nothing was certain the world today and ditching a career he loved for a woman who only captivated him was not an option. Yet, he couldn't bring himself to walk away from the female who could go from stunning model to badass cop in the blink of an eye. There was something between them and he wasn't ready to give up on it. If they were careful, if they snuck around and kept things as platonic as they could, maybe it would help him move his own decision along.

"You're not going to like this."

The sound of Chase's voice coming from behind him startled Jeremy. He hadn't realized how much time had passed. His friend appeared and sat down on the edge of his desk.

"He won't remove me from training?"

"Oh, he's ordered your ass off. Scolded me a bit for not seeing the sexual tension in the room, like I'm some sort of sniffing dog or something. You're not to go anywhere near O'Casey. Not in the office or out. He's given you a nice ultimatum. Keep it in your pants, or take the DEA offer and turn in your gun and badge now, – not when you're ready to start over there."

Jeremy nodded. The words angered him. He knew there was nothing he could do and it made things all the more difficult. He'd always followed every single rule, even during his destructive pursuit last year. He'd never expected the captain to rule so harshly on something that wasn't the worst Internal Affairs issue to ever happen in any precinct.

"I've got a class to get to. You're my friend, Jeremy, one of the best ones I've got, and sure as shit, the best partner I ever had. But I'm staying out of this one. I'm advising you to think with your badge right now. This is the life you left Montgomery for. Don't piss it away for a girl you like fucking."

Chase didn't wait for Jeremy's response. He pushed past Jeremy and walked out the door to get to the class of recruits he'd kept waiting to help Jeremy deal with this problem. He wasn't certain if he was angry with Chase for his utter lack of support as a friend, or because he'd reduced Bridget to nothing more than a hook-up. He was angry with his friend and his captain, but oddly enough, not himself.

Jeremy's hands curled into fists. He uncurled them as he forced himself to calm down. Bridget O'Casey might just be the perfect woman. They were going to see what they had together, even if it meant lying to everyone he'd worked with for the past ten years.

Bridget blinked as she looked down at the score on the paper. "Ninety-eight," she whispered the words as if they were sacred as the rest of the group patiently rose when their names were called to grab theirs.

The exam wasn't anything terribly serious, but rather more of a gauging system. To see the almost perfect score shining back at her made it hard to keep herself from grinning. A sideways glance at Ashley's paper told her that her friend had secured a score in the mid-eighties. Bridget was happy that for once she hadn't excelled too far past Ashley.

Things had been such a whirlwind for the past few weeks after Jeremy had gone to the captain she was shocked she'd managed to keep up.

Jeremy had somehow spoken with Captain. It had resulted in both of them being called into his office for a reprimand for not speaking out on day one. They'd been issued, a warning to not to let it happen ever again. The next day, Jeremy had been replaced by Santana, a vice cop. For a week, they had attempted to fully ignore one another again. Like the last time, it ended with her showing up on his doorstep with a pair of regulation cuffs she'd snagged from his car on her way to the door.

From then out she and Jeremy didn't even try to play by the new rules. Which may have been foolish but neither of them had been willing to put their lives on hold if they could succeed in getting around the system, just until Jeremy made his career choice. They made damn certain to not be seen anywhere near one another inside the big precinct area, which left them staying in most nights.

The past few weeks had been difficult. She'd been splitting her time between cramming sessions with Ashley and Marcus, to sneaking around with Jeremy. Since then, their relationship had been nothing if not

Boy Scout and Girl Scout clean. Minus the fact that it was still against regulation to be seeing one another in any fashion. Most nights, she stayed at his place till it got late and then he would drive her back to her own home. They'd alternated between him incessantly quizzing her to cooking dinner together in his kitchen. They felt like a couple. Even her body was screaming for them to do more than cook.

"O'Casey, are you with us, recruit?"

Chase's voice snapped her out of her thoughts of Jeremy. She whipped her head up wards, a flush of color darkening her cheeks.

"Yes, sir. Forgive me, sir."

She thought she caught the briefest glimpse of a smile on his lips, but it disappeared as quickly as it apeared.

"Scores like that don't mean you can daydream in my classroom. How well do you think that would go over if you were with Juarez and Santana? Not well, is the correct answer. Head out of the clouds. You've still got three weeks to go. I will not tolerate a swelled head. Ego gets cops killed."

The last sentence bounced around in her ears, like the echo from a microphone, and she sunk down into her chair. He was right, she was behaving appallingly. Sooner or later, these daydreams of Jeremy were going to get her into serious trouble. The new year was closing in fast, and he hadn't made a single mention about his placement with or without the DEA – not that she had any real business in knowing.

That didn't make hearing the words any easier. On top of essentially breaking every rule by being with a cop, the one person who needed to like her thought she was a boastful toad.

Fantastic.

"All available units, I repeat, all available units. There is a 10-53 on the south side steps of the San Diego precinct. All available units please report now."

The static crackle of the police scanner they used to listen to some days went off in the corner behind Chase. The room went utterly silent. Bridget felt bile rising in the back of her throat. No one was speaking around her and the words were out of her mouth before she could hold them back.

"That's not a practice code, is it?" her voice trembled as she asked and she could feel the fear coursing through her body go straight down to her toes.

Chase's body language told her everything she needed to know before he'd even opened his mouth to answer. She could see it in the way the muscles in his neck tensed, and in the way he ground his teeth together. Her eyes dropped to his fisted hands and she felt herself gag.

"No one move. Everyone remain here and stay off your phones." Chase barked the command so loudly she flinched as he ran out the door.

The minute the door closed behind him a cacophony of voices broke out amongst the thirty-eight recruits gathered in the small room. Only she couldn't make sense of anything that was being said. Her eyes had gone back to the silent scanner, no longer making noise because. Chase had switched it off as he'd raced out. Another shooting had occurred, this time almost two hours away. Yet, she felt as if it had been someone close to her the scanner was talking about.

The sensation of ants walking all over her broke out and her skin crawled as her mind flashed to Jeremy. She knew he would be completely safe, He wasn't out in the filed because of his punishment. However, all she wanted to do was bolt up from her chair and run through the stairwells until she made it the fifth floor where his desk was to see him. Her heart pounded so hard within her chest, she swore she could hear it in her ears.

"Bridget. Bridget!" Ashley's shaking voice breached her own thoughts, and she swiveled to look at her friend.

Tears threatened to fall down her cheeks, her face was ashen white and her lower lip trembled with the effort of holding herself in check. Though her voice sounded completely calm, she was anything but that. That's when it hit Bridget. Ashley's brother had transferred down to the SDPD so that she could have a shot here, which meant Ashley was a ticking time bomb.

"Hey, hey, don't think about it. Just breathe deeply. Don't text him, don't call him. We have no idea what kind of lockdown they would have gone into. If you don't hear from him, your brain will come up with the worst possible scenarios. Promise me you won't touch the phone."

Ashley barley nodded her head. A single tear slipped down her cheek, smudging the makeup she had on. Bridget's own heart constricted. Her father had never faced anything like this while he was active, but he'd been shot down outside a known police hangout. She'd been through this, even if she'd been three thousand miles away. She'd called his phone a million times after her mother called, and he never answered. He couldn't of course.

"What she said. Let's do something to take your mind off of it. No studying, no hanging out in the cafeteria while drinking coffee and watching the cops mull about trying to figure out what they're working on either. I'll call my brother and see if we can get three of his best day's haul. We'll take a nice trip to Long Beach and I'll show you ladies that a surfer and ex- fisherman-turned- cop can cook a mean meal."

Marcus had walked up behind Ashley and was slowly massaging her shoulders. Despite everything, Bridget couldn't help but to smile. She was either watching the most bizarre couple come together, or seeing Marcus at his finest because he certainly hadn't been so understanding with Bridget last month when she'd freaked out herself. Either way, she was happy Ashley had someone supporting her right now.

"Listen up," Chase's voice rang out above all the chattering, and the slamming door sent a wave of quiet through the room. "This is not an event that is to be shared. Details have not been released to the media. If we find out any recruit has voluntarily, or accidentally, shared information with the media, there will be worse consequences than being removed from the academy. Keep that in mind. This is a delicate situation, and there is reason for us to shut down for the day. Enjoy your weekend and remember, this job is about doing well. Do not let the fear of these shootings take that away. If there is a connection, the stations will find it. Either way, the killers will be behind bars soon enough."

No one spoke as they gathered their belongings and packed away the papers Chase had passed out minutes earlier. The air was heavy with disdain and nervousness. When she stood and walked past Chase, she felt the barest touch on her wrist and stopped walking. When her eyes met his, she saw the warning in them and she gasped. He was letting her know he knew her secret and didn't approve.

A lick of anger raced through her. She pulled herself away and continued out the door if she wasn't to avoid saying anything to Chase. Jeremy had told him, and he hadn't brought down the wrath of the department, then he was trustworthy. She couldn't begrudge Jeremy for having someone to talk to. She'd told Ashley and Marcus not too long ago herself.

That didn't mean she liked the warning in Chase's eyes. It made her all the more anxious to get to Jeremy and talk to him but she could tell Chase was simply letting her know she shouldn't go to him for comfort.

When Marcus pushed open the door to the lot, she

was shocked to find Jeremy leaning against his car and parked directly next to Marcus' car. Jeremy's blue eyes locked onto her eyes from across the way and she felt her body blaze to life. The intensity of his gaze both troubled and excited her.

His eyes narrowed at her and he was hunched over. The muscles in his forearms looked like they would burst through his uniform with how hard he was crossing his arms over his chest. The typical smirk on his lips was replaced by a scowl and he looked so dark and dangerous. She couldn't stop herself from thinking about what he would be like in bed like this.

"Looks like someone needs a rain check on the fish," Marcus joked good-naturedly.

Bridget opened her mouth to tell him to knock it off when she felt Jeremy's hand slide over hers. The heat from his hand warmed her in ways she couldn't ignore. Panicking, she looked about to be sure they weren't watched. The parking lot wasn't empty. Officers leaned against patrol cars, and recruits filed out of the building and were getting into their cars.

Jeremy was taking an unnecessary risk, as if he needed to assure himself she was ok. The way his eyes locked onto her lips she could almost already feel his mouth pressed against hers. But he didn't kiss her, it was all in her mind.

A low growl escaped him as he tugged her a step away from Ashley. "Let me take you home and stay the night at your place tonight."

A shiver coursed through her as she thought about the reasons he would want to, and his voice was an un-sensual as it could be. Which meant this was about protecting her, wanting to assure himself that she was safe. It sent a thrill through her, to know how serious they were becoming about one another, and all without any other sexual interactions. Her whole body buzzed, coming alive with the knowledge that they were something to one another, that she wasn't the only one under some sort of spell.

"Yes."

The word was laced with more subtext than she'd meant for it to be and she just stared as he let her hand go and got into the car.

Bridget was torn between jumping in after him and checking out who might be watching them. She had no clue as to whether he'd made a career decision, but after the look Chase gave had given her on the way out, she was going to protect him until she knew for certain.

The passenger door opened from the inside. Jeremy leaned over the seat, his eyes focused on hers.

"Are you getting in or not?" The growl in his voice was more prominent, and the scowl on his face deepened.

She'd upset him by stalling. Quickly, she slid into the passenger seat and closed the door. His face was so close to hers that she couldn't stop as she turned and pressed her lips to his. His hands came up to her cheeks and held her face as his tongue pushed into her mouth and claimed her.

When he pulled away they were both breathing hard. Neither one apologized for the foolishness of what they'd just done.

"Don't ask me why. Just let me hold you tonight. There's something more going on with these shooting's and whether or not we're dating, I need to know you're with me tonight."

He pulled away and focused on the road as he backed out of his parking spot. Her body trembled as a combination of need and fear coursed through her veins. This big, strong man wanted to keep her safe. While she loved the thought of it, a part of her feared what could make him so on edge.

"I didn't mean to scare you just now." Jeremy spoke after a few minutes of driving in silence. "I just don't want you to be alone tonight."

Bridget turned her head from looking out the window and smiled at him. He felt so much in that smile. It evoked feelings within him he never thought possible. It killed him that they had to act like this, keeping everything a secret as they snuck around.

In his hard of hearts Jeremy wasn't quite ready to accept the DEA's offer just yet. It was a big deal and he wanted to be certain he was doing the right thing.

But the more he looked at Bridget, the more he started to wonder if the right thing wasn't to put something before his career, just this once.

If the shootings kept up, there was a damned good chance he'd throw caution to the wind and take what he'd been offered with the DEA. He and Juarez had been screwing around by the coffee machine outside Captain Danvers' office when the bulletin had broken out.

He'd been ready to say fuck it all and dash downstairs to make sure Bridget was safe and sound. The captain had then barked a command over the phone to get the recruits out of the building. Jeremy had been on the verge of busting in and asking to work as a liaison with the two counties that had been attacked and rescuing Bridget.

Deep inside, he'd chosen her, probably had awhile ago but this moment painted the picture of how important she was so vividly he couldn't ignore it if he wanted to. Her father had been shot, and she'd been left alone to deal with it on her own. He hadn't been there for her after the last shooting because he'd been too busy trying to follow the letter of the law himself. This time, however, he wouldn't let her cope with it alone.

"Something in me just snapped. I needed to touch you, to hold you and confirm that you were actually in that damned basement and not in San Diego." The words sounded foolish as he said them.

"I had the same feeling. I knew you were safe upstairs, that you were working on some other case, but I just wanted to go up and see you."

The words comforted him a bit but he wondered why she hadn't done so. "So why didn't you?"

"I didn't want to put your job on the line. It was foolish to worry. I know how important your reputation is to you. Plus, Chase let me know he knows about us as we were leaving. I got the distinct impression he disapproves."

"Screw Chase. He's my closest friend, so he's only thinking about the job and me. Not me and my heart. I've been engaged before. It ended because I was too wrapped up in an investigation. I made Chase promise to keep me on the straight and narrow after that. No women before work and no women who didn't seem to understand my work either. He's just holding up his end of the bargain."

She nodded, but the purse of her lips told him she didn't agree or care. If she was curious about his engagement, she didn't ask. They drove the rest of the way to her town house just outside the main city border in silence. He liked it out here. It was close enough to have the action, but also far enough away when the day was done, she could come home and spend some time in her peaceful backyard.

Hell of a long drive to make in silence though.

He parked the vehicle and turned to look at her. "Are we ok? About my telling Chase? I needed someone to understand the situation to get me out of the training and he was my partner before and like a brother now."

"We're fine. I'm sorry. I have no right to be angry with him. I just, I don't know where we stand, Jeremy and I don't know up from down right now."

She sighed and he felt awful.

Every fiber of him his being screamed to tell her he'd take the DEA's offer, and maybe after tonight he would. He knew how he felt about her but he wouldn't put a woman before his career, not even a wonderful one. *Isn't that already what you're doing sneaking around?* He thought as he got out and opened the door for her, extending his hand to help her out.

"I know you can't understand everything, but thank you for willing to be in this…this half of a relationship with me."

He kissed her lightly on the forehead and left his lips there. Jeremy could feel her smile by the way her muscles moved beneath his lips.

"How about you make it up to me tonight by cooking that famous leg of lamb you keep boasting about?"

He laughed as she unlocked the door to her house. "I take it you were planning this all along for the next time I was over and have all the needed ingredients?"

She grinned back at him and winked, all the tension gone between them. "My, my, you are a good detective, aren't you?"

He playfully swatted her ass as she closed the door. Bridget turned and wrapped her arms around his neck, but she didn't kiss him. His blood was pumping so fast through his body he swore he saw stars from being so turned on.

"This is going to kill me, Bridget. You're going to kill me."

She chuckled and unwound her hands. "Sorry, I know we can't. Not again. Not yet…" Her voice trailed off, and for the third time that afternoon, he wanted to break down and give into what they both wanted.

"How about that lamb now? An early dinner? It takes a good four hours to cook anyway."

He tried to ease out of the situation and the way she took a step back from him killed a little piece of him. It was needed, though. The way things were going, he knew more and more he was leaning towards the DEA position for the right reasons– not just for the money or woman in the room with him.

"Dear god. I have to wait to kiss you, and now I have to wait to be fed? Not fair, Trellins. Not even slightly fair." she joked.

She tossed her hair behind her after ripping out the elastic tie that had been holding it in place. Jeremy he itched to run his fingers through it, but he ignored the notion. He ignored every part of him that wanted to kiss her while they cooked and while they ate dinner. Five hours together had left enough sexual energy in the room for him to come undone from it alone and no actual touching. He yearned to push things to another level between them, as he did every time they had a night like this.

They soon found themselves sitting on the couch with a glass of wine in hand. Bridget's legs were draped casually over his.

"So, in light of all the decision making, I have to ask," she took a small sip of the red wine and a line dribbled down her chin. Jeremy wanted to lick it off her, but forced himself to sit still, curious as to what her question was and knowing how dangerous that action would have been. "Why did you become a cop so far from home?"

He sighed and took a long swig from his own wine glass. Jeremy hated talking about back home and it was the only subject they'd shied away from in the past month and a half.

"I wanted to get out of my parent's grasp." Truth, but limited.

She pushed herself off the couch and sat upright as she faced him. "And just what might that mean, Mister Super Secretive Alabama Man?"

He chuckled at her and brushed a hand over her shoulder. "It means my parents are extremely wealthy and if I wanted to make something in my name, I needed to move."

If she cared about his admission that he had money she didn't show it.

"The secrets come out tonight, don't they?" She winked. "Your brother and sister, they stayed because it was easy for them there, then?"

"Precisely. Stepping into Daddy's law firm would have been a piece of cake for any of us. Thomas works as a lawyer, and Susan is in the accounting department. Neither of them had the guts to try on their own. Why would they with the paycheck my dad offered?"

"Because you did."

If he wasn't mistaken, he heard pride for him in her voice, and it made him smile.

"Being the oldest just meant that I was used as a cautionary tale. Including running off to the City of Angels and taking up something dangerous. I just wanted to be my own person, even if just for a little while. But I fell in love with the job." He titled his head sideways and gave her a lopsided smile. "I don't think I need to explain that part to you, though."

She laughed. He loved the way her face lit up, how there was no trace of the fear she'd felt from earlier.

"But why LA? Why not some place smaller?"

He took another drink of his wine and set the empty glass on her coffee table. "I wanted crime. I wanted a place where I'd actually be doing more than

141

writing parking tickets and the NYPD was too much of a stretch, so I chose here."

She nodded and he could see the look in her eyes, the lust and need lurking in their depths. All he had to do was lean close to her, and push aside everything that stopped them from doing what they wanted to do. She was ready, and if opening up about his family to someone other than Chase meant anything, so was he. DEA job or not, he didn't want to hide from the relationship behind the excuse of following the rules. Because that's all the stalling was, hiding from the fear of her being just like the others he had dated and tearing him apart.

Bridget pulled herself back first and grabbed the remote. She turned the TV on and he heard the wine glass shatter as it hit the coffee table a moment later. Immediately, he pulled himself away from his thoughts and directed his eyes to the TV.

"That's right, Mary. I'm standing in front of the fountain where the bodies of three police officers were removed earlier today. The area has been completely cleaned and a an inconclusive sweep for prints was done. The commissioner has yet to issue any statements but three lives were lost today in this tragedy. It begs the question, are these shootings connected?"

He leaned forward and yanked the remote a little abruptly from her hand, promptly hitting the power button. The clean image of the SDPD vanished from the screen as it went black; but not before he could feel Bridget shaking against him. He wrapped his arms around her, hoping to offer her a bit of comfort. Her head found its way to his chest, and he gently ran his hand over the back of her head.

"Just ignore it, Darlin'. Focus on the sound of my voice. It's late anyway. Let me take you to bed. Just to bed. I meant what I said earlier. I want to hold you tonight, to know your safe."

Her lower lip trembled. She bit down on it so hard, it turned white, and he cringed at how much it must have hurt. Bridget nodded and pulled back from him to stand up. When she stretched her hand behind her indicating for him to take it, he wasted no time in gripping it and standing up.

As they walked up the stairs he couldn't ignore the way her shoulders were tight with tension. Without thinking, he placed a kiss between her shoulder blades. She tensed and then her shoulders relaxed.

"You're safe, Bridget. I'm safe. Everyone down here is safe. Let's just get some sleep."

He'd meant the words to be a comfort to her as they rounded the doorway into her bedroom. Whether they were or weren't, he didn't know, but when she pulled the covers back and lay down, he climbed in next to her and pulled her body against his. If this was what happiness was like, there wasn't a shadow of a doubt in his mind that he was going to take the DEA job first thing Monday morning.

He laid his head on the extra pillow, and she snuggled against him. His body didn't react with the usual surge of lust. Instead, he smiled as the smell of her citrus shampoo reached his nose. He ran a hand over her side before wrapping his arm around her.

"Goodnight, Bridget.

7

Trevor couldn't help the shiver of satisfaction he felt as he pulled the trigger. The booming sound of the gun was silenced by the pillows he shot into. It had seemed impossible to pull a man from the steps of the SDPD, but it hadn't been. His old crew had stepped in to help out, and the five person shooting team had done a number on the police.

Prior to starting, he'd made sure Michael, the sixth guy, had a van hot wired and ready to go on the side of the street. The best part of almost any city, there was always sidewalk parking. This one happened to have it surrounding all four sides of the building, which the task at hand a breeze.

Trevor fired another shot into the pillow he had tied over the female cop's other knee. Her scream was

145

muffled by the pillow he'd duck tapped around her head as well. The sound was loud enough that he felt a pang of lust grip him from her pain.

"You see, I didn't kill a cop on purpose. But I am now."

He lunged forward and yanked the pillow from her face. The tape tore a portion of her hair from her head. Tears streamed down her face when she looked at him. It made him feel even more powerful.

Blood coursed down her knees and dripped onto the floor beneath the chair she was tied to. The socks stuffed and taped to her mouth prevented her from making too much noise. Trevor supposed that the pillow could have killed her, but it hadn't and he was going to anyway so it didn't exactly matter.

He walked over to the makeshift desk and picked up the knife. He sliced a section of his thumb, testing its sharpness, and grinned as he turned back to her.

"See, it's like I kept telling them. I hadn't done a damned thing wrong back then. I spent all that time in jail for no fucking reason."

He moved forward and traced the blade down her

neck. A thin, beaded, blood red line appeared across her flesh. She whimpered and he felt even more powerful.

He dragged the backside of the blade over her throat as he pulled the tape free of her lips. Trevor kissed her neck and whispered into her ear.

"Now, now, Cheryl, don't worry. I did like you all those times you brought my dinner. I'll make this quick for you and I'll make certain your body isn't just dumped in a trash pile back in San Diego. I'll have them arrange your body all nice like."

She whimpered and for a moment, the scared teenage boy grabbed hold of his mind and the hand holding the knife shook. But this was the way he wanted to do things. If they were going to hold him for killing cops, he was damned sure going to kill cops. When they were done, the seven of them could go someplace on the other side of the country, hook up once they got there, and focus on being good citizens.

If you can stop remembering how damned good it feels to spill blood. The thought pulled him away from the scared version of himself that had been incarcerated years ago.

"Sorry again."

In a quick motion, he flipped the knife so that the sharpened edge was pressed against her throat at yanked it across her throat. She didn't scream out as he sliced into her flesh. Trevor shivered with excitement as the warm blood slid over his hands. If this was how much better it felt to kill up close, versus a shot from a gun, they may have to steal someone from each of the remaining five counties.

Cheryl's head dropped to her chest, lolling and lifeless. He wiped the knife off on her shirt, and grabbed his faithful Sharpie from his pants pocket, drawing a big "X" over San Diego's dot on the wall map. Trevor then pulled the latex gloves he had on off and shoved them into his pocket along with the marker. The knife he dropped onto the ground. Even if someone found this place, all that they would find was the location. None of his prints would be found.

It would be dark now, well past nine at night. He kicked open the door of the small shack. The two men waiting outside were startled by the door swinging open and he scoffed.

"Man the fuck up. Let's get the car over here. It's done. I promised her we'd take her back to San Diego and drop her some place nice."

He put his hands in his pocket and fingered the gloves stuffed inside each pocket.

His revenge was feeling awfully good.

Bridget stretched her arms above her head as she slowly opened her eyes. Light filtered in through the plantation shutters over her windows. A yawn escaped her. She could still feel Jeremy's hand draped over her waist and it made her smile. They' had been very careful not to sleep in the same bed over the past few months, the temptation too great.

However, she couldn't think of anything that felt better than right now, than waking up still in his arms. Bridget should have felt emotionally drained from learning about yet another police attack. She should have even been riled up from the lack of sexual activities between them. Instead, she simply felt content and well rested.

"This is something I could certainly get used too." she whispered to no one at all.

Jeremy's body twitched a little and she froze, not wanting to wake him before he was ready. She knew he only had today off because he'd initially been slated for training schedule. Bridget wanted to let him enjoy his sleep.

A buzz sounded in the room. She flinched as her cell phone continued to ring on her nightstand.

"Well, there went letting him sleep."

Bridget leaned over, slowly rolling out from under his arm, and grabbed the phone. Marcus' name popped up on the device's screen. She wrinkled her nose, debating if she should pick it up. What if something was wrong with Ashley?

Her finger jabbed the ignore button on the screen. She then pulled up a text message instead.

"What's up? Can't talk, atm."

"You could have taken that call," a groggy voice said from behind her, startling her, as she hadn't expected him to be awake despite the buzz.

Bridget rolled around to face him and found herself staring into his light blue eyes. He looked sleepy, though his eyes held a hint of playfulness. Without thinking, she pressed her lips against his, and his arms wrapped around her body.

The kiss grew passionate between them. They were in no rush to go anywhere, content with the moment they shared together. Until Jeremy pulled back.

"You are a temptation I can't avoid much longer, Bridget."

She smiled at him, even as a small pang of guilt wrapped itself around her. She'd never intended for him to break his code of ethics, but she wouldn't push him away, or be the bigger person and walk away from him either.

"Well, when you're ready, I'll be here."

Her phone vibrated again, and she figured it was Marcus. She sat up and grabbed the device again, happy to see that the message on the screen wasn't anything disastrous.

"Looks like the surf is good today over in Seal Beach. Marcus and Ashley are surfing and asked me to come along. If you want to join"

She responded that she would be there, wondering if they would mind if he came too.

Bridget wasn't certain why she told him. She was unsure if she wanted his permission to go, or if she wanted him to tell her to stay in bed with him. Maybe she wanted him to want to come too. He smiled at her, but didn't take the bait she'd dangled before him.

"Do you surf?"

She wrinkled her nose at him, not wanting to look too desperate, so she didn't push the subject of him actually addressing the invitation. "Not very well, but I learned when I was in high school."

He sat up too and tugged her so she was cuddled against him. "Do you like to surf?"

She smiled as she cozied up to him and inhaled his scent. "I love the ocean. I also love not having a huge hunk of wood, plastic, or fiberboard slam into my head or choke on salt water. But I wouldn't say I hate surfing."

He laid his chin on the top of her head. "Hmm, so you would be up for taking them up on this Saturday outing of theirs?"

She felt him smirk because of where his chin was and wanted to playfully elbow him for being such a man. Instead, she pulled away from him and stood up out of bed, stretching her arms above her head again. Her sleep sweater slipped upwards, exposing the bare flesh of her stomach.

His eyes followed the lift of her sweater, landing on her black boy shorts. She didn't sleep with any pants on. He let out a low growl, and she couldn't help but to laugh.

"You know what, I think I will go. I could use some sun on this pale skin of mine. No more spray tans and airbrushing the white away." It didn't matter that she'd already told Marcus she would.

She turned towards her dresser, biting her lower lip. *Ask Jeremy, just fucking ask already!* She thought as she rummaged through the middle drawer for her favorite green one piece.

He cleared his throat from behind her. "Would you be opposed if maybe I tagged along? I think I'd like to be in public with you. If the two of them already know our half secret, well Seal Beach certainly wouldn't have anyone to recognize us." His sexy southern accent had an almost awkward tone to it and she wondered if she turned, if he would be blushing. Which would be incredibly sexy but she doubted he would like her seeing him do that.

Bridget smirked and quickly wiped it off her face before turning around with her green bathing suit in hand. "I can't think of anything I would like more. But are you certain?" She hadn't meant to ask the last part, but it was too late.

Jeremy didn't hesitate in answering, and she sighed in relief. "I'm positive. I want to see what we can have if we aren't just sitting around cooking and talking, or having killer sex." He winked at her.

Bridget pulled the sweater off and walked towards the adjacent bathroom. "Well, in that case, you'd better go get yourself a bathing suit."

Jeremy noticed the look of utter alarm on Marcus' face as they stepped out of Bridget's car and for a moment, he wanted to turn around and pretend like he was just dropping her off. Asking to come along had been impulsive. She'd been hinting at it, and he'd taken the bait. He was well and truly tired of faking a relationship with her and the more he got to know her, the more he knew taking the DEA job was the right course of action for him to take. So why not spend a day and see her truly having fun instead of being holed up inside a house?

Just as the strange sensation of insecurity wrapped itself around him tightly enough to make him want to bolt backward, Bridget's hand slipped inside his. His trepidation went away as quickly as the look on Marcus's face had put it there.

The sand felt warm beneath his feet. They'd left their flip-flops in the car because Bridget said nothing was better than sand in between the toes. Ashley's face beamed the closer they got to her. He wondered just how many details Bridget had shared with her closest friends at the station.

"You brought a tagalong, huh?" Ashley's voice was light-hearted, and she gave a whimsical sounding laugh.

Marcus crossed his arms over his chest, and eyed Jeremy up and down before he smiled. Jeremy liked it. He felt like Marcus was the big brother giving him a once-over. The idea that Bridget had someone looking out for her like that pleased him. Especially seeing as how Marcus seemed to show a sign of approval.

"Seems she did. Hope you two don't mind."

Jeremy pulled his sunglasses off his face, sliding them to the top of his head. He offered them what Bridget called his charming side smirk.

"Not at all. Though, won't this cause some problems for you on the job?" Marcus asked as they turned and started walking toward a little setup on the sand.

He sucked in a deep breath and he felt Bridget squeeze his hand a little. "It certainly will. But you two won't say anything. I've been assured of that. We're far enough away from the area that no one should recognize me and cause problems."

Jeremy pulled his shirt over his head as they stopped in front of the stuff that must have belonged to Ashley and Marcus. Marcus looked like he was biting his lip to keep himself from asking more. Jeremy nodded, turning his attention to Bridget as she pulled the light purple sundress over her head. He hadn't even realized she'd let his hand go. His eyes traveled over her body. She laughed as their gazes clashed. He smirked at her and shrugged.

"You're very lucky you're cute, do you know that?" she said.

She laughed as she said it and he had an overwhelming urge to tug her to him and kiss her. An urge that was difficult to ignore but he did for the time being.

"So, where do we get the boards?" Ashley asked, changing the subject and breaking the sexual tension that had been fizzling between them.

Marcus laughed. "Such newbies! Can any of you even surf?"

"I can, smartass, not well, but I can. This one, though . . ." Bridget jerked a thumb at Jeremy, "he's from the Midwest, so you never know."

Jeremy playfully kicked sand at her at the same time that Ashley admitted to never being on a board. He'd been surfing plenty, but he figured there was no reason to tell her and ruin her pretty farm boy image of him. It was so much better to simply shock her when they got out on the surf.

"There's a rental shack about a five minute walk that way." Marcus pointed to the strip of beach to the left of them. "Why not take our stuff and move over there? It'll be easier than lugging the boards back and forth for the little pixies."

Jeremy couldn't help but laugh, he felt Bridget playfully slap him at the same time that Ashley landed one on Marcus's forearm.

"We're going to show you two, aren't we, Bridget?" Ashley chimed.

Bridget's eyes narrowed and her mouth curved into a wicked smile. "Oh, I should say so. Just not out here, but on the training course. I can think of a way or two to take them down." She laughed and the two girls started to walk away. "For now, let's just let the big strong men carry all the stuff."

Jeremy shook his head and chuckled as he and Marcus bent down to grab their clothes, cooler, and shoes. "They do this to you often? Make you the muscle?"

"Ha. Not a chance, normally those two are out to prove they're more of a man than I am any chance they can get. So far, they don't have too much luck, but damn, can Bridget out-fucking-shoot me any day of the week in classes."

Jeremy couldn't help the grin of pride he felt for Bridget. "She sure is something."

"She sure is, which is why I don't think you ought to make too much of a habit out of coming around like this. Unless there's some sort of way this all works out." Marcus said coolly.

The polite threat hung between them and Jeremy looked up to make sure the girls were far enough away from them. He respected Marcus for this. Chase had damned near done the same thing a month and a half ago, but he didn't need some virtual stranger telling him how to do things.

"I'm not certain it's any of your business, Marcus. But I'd be willing to hear you explain how it is till we grab the boards."

"The way I see it, Bridget is not only a training partner, but like a kid sister. She's realizing her full potential and honoring her father. But she's new, just starting out. Then there's you—a golden cop and so stuck to the rulebook. I've heard people joke about you marrying it. So, in my mind, not only does it not make sense for a guy like you to pursue her, but it also stands to reason that should you get caught, she's the one in danger of losing everything. Not you."

Marcus' voice held little anger but Jeremy had a feeling the laid back ex-fisherman was giving it to him pretty good.

"I don't think I have to explain my relationship with her to you. But, if it will make some of this go away and make it a nice day for her, then I will. We tried to start something before we realized who the other one was career wise. I stopped it, like an utter ass. It didn't last. We have fun together. We care about each other in a way that feels so natural. Ignoring it feels like I'm denying a part of myself. We're doing our best to keep it casual, but after two months, or practically two, I don't want to keep it casual anymore. Do I want to put our jobs on the line? Fuck no, but sometimes, there are some things too important to ignore and for me this is one of them."

He turned his head to look at Marcus and was shocked to see the man practically grinning from ear to ear.

"Now that is something this older man likes to hear. I may have spent my life loving the sea but it doesn't mean I can't appreciate a good old sap story when I hear one. Trust me, I've heard her pine over you more than once ever since she was called out by Ashley. She's just as serious as you are. Question is, what are you going to do if it gets really serious?"

He could feel the warm sand slip between his toes as Marcus asked the question. Again, none of this was really Marcus's business, but maybe having someone else to talk to about it was a good thing. Someone that knew Bridget outside her abilities and potential as an officer, and had her best interests at heart.

"I've been offered a job at the DEA, working the Southern California circuit. If I take it, it would open up every door working as a detective keeps closed." He held up his hand before Marcus could say anything. "I know you're going to ask why I haven't taken it. The answer is simple; I didn't want to change everything for a girl I'd just met. Now though, after a few months, I'm pretty certain there's no course of action except to take the job. Today is sort of the test run for that idea, since we've never done anything in public together."

"Test run?" Bridget's voice sounded more than slightly irked.

Jeremy looked up, shocked that they'd caught up to the girls and the rental shack. He felt as his cheeks flamed red and he rubbed the back of his neck, embarrassed by the fact that he'd been overheard.

"Umm…"

"Don't umm me, buddy. Just keep in mind that now I'm going to be twice as hard to please today." She turned towards Marcus. "And you, Mr. I-Think-I'm-Her-Brother," She paused and Jeremy was certain Marcus was going to get it. "Thank you for looking out for me."

Jeremy blinked rapidly, surprised by how it all worked out and the others laughed. "I'm never going to try and understand a woman. Are you three done talking and ready to get some waves?"

Marcus high-fived him and even Ashley nodded. "Well then, guess we better get out there."

They paid for the boards for the day. Jeremy was the first to take off running. The cold water splashed up his legs and onto his bare stomach. He flinched a little, but threw himself down on the board and began to paddle out.

It had been some time since he'd been out on the waves. Work was often too all consuming. The cold water splashed and invaded his mouth as he paddled out and sat up on the board. He could see the trio standing at the water's edge staring at him. He laughed and turned to watch the swells.

The water was calmer than normal today, perfect for a newbie like Ashley, but a little boring for him. So he sat there and waited. When the fifth wave crashed against his back, he let out a low whistle at the one coming in. He got ready and stood up at the right moment. The thrill of the wave caught him, and he let out a whoop as he wobbled a little on the board.

He'd forgotten how just goofing off could feel, and he knew he owed Bridget a thank you for this. The wave swooped him back towards the shore, sending everything into a blur. It was a great rush, but he wasn't paying attention to his footing and slipped backward.

Water crashed over his head. His eyes snapped shut even as he prayed for the board not to slam down on top of him. Jeremy felt his ass slam into the sand on the ocean floor, the jolt vibrating through his body. He'd been in shallow enough water before during a wipeout and he pushed off the ground with his feet. His head easily broke the surface and he gasped, taking even more water into his mouth because he hadn't fully stood up.

Jeremy sputtered for air as Bridget swam to his side.

"Are you ok?" Concern laced her voice and he stood upright fully as she spoke. "I didn't know you could do that! Or maybe you couldn't, given your less than expert dismount." she teased.

Bridget reached her hand down to him. Jeremy grasped it and jerked her into the water next to him. She shrieked, probably from the shock of cold fully covering her now, and splashed water at him. He laughed and grinned at her, splashing water back at her and hitting Ashley as she waded out to them.

"I got cocky, that's all."

Bridget stood up and playfully kicked some water at him. "Cocky and jerky, pulling me into the water like that when I just came to see if you're all right."

"Not going to offer me a hand again?" He smirked at her and pushed himself up all the way once more, making more than just his chest break the shallow three-foot water.

"Not on your life, mister."

"Not a bad run till the end. I didn't know the Midwest knew what to do with water outside their showers." Marcus laughed and grabbed Jeremy's board as it floated by.

"Oh, there's a lot us midwestern boys can do. But that, well, I've been out here almost ten years. I've learned a lot. You might even mistake me for a local."

"Minus that sexy southern accent that caused me to let you buy me a drink that night." Bridget joked.

"Aha, I knew it wasn't my good looks that got you into bed. I have been told my accent charms a woman's panties off."

He smirked and this time she and Ashley both rolled their eyes at him.

"If you two are done, is someone going to teach me how to surf or what?" Ashley asked.

"If she doesn't mind, I'd like to talk to Bridget real quick. Marcus is probably the better teacher anyway."

Marcus slid the surfboard across the water to him. "Damn straight I am. Let's go, Ashley. Let's see how you handle paddling out."

Jeremy offered Bridget a hand as they waded back to the sand and Ashley and Marcus grabbed their boards. The sand stuck instantly to his wet feet and he cringed as it glued itself to his legs when they settled down to talk on their sandy towels. He slipped his hand into hers and laced their fingers together once they were alone. It was damned near impossible to ignore the charge he felt when he touched her. He didn't want to anymore either.

He looked into her eyes and smoothed the wet, dark hair off her forehead with his free hand. Their eyes were locked together and he could fell the desire pounding inside of him from the barest contact of their hands together. He could feel his body hardening and almost groaned. Jeremy slid a little closer to her, their wet bodies molding together so perfectly.

He did groan softly at the contact.

Jeremy lowered his head, lowered and his lips pressed them against hers before either of them had said anything to stop it. She tasted like saltwater and he didn't care one bit. Her body came to life against his immediately. She ran her tongue over his lower lip, and slipped it inside his mouth as he opened his lips for her. Their tongues danced and slid against each other's, slippery and perfect just the same as they explored every nook and cranny.

The kiss set both of them on fire if how she moved to sit in his lap was any indication of her desire, he could just tell. Bridget ran her hands up and down his back before squeezing his shoulders and locking her hands around his neck. Jeremy cupped her ass, pulling her further against him, not caring as to whom else the hell was watching. Captain Danvers could have rolled up and nothing would have mattered to him but the woman in his arms.

"Beach." she gasped when he finally pulled back. "We're on a public beach."

Her voice was shaking with lust. Her lips were swollen, red and pouty from his kiss and he fucking loved the way it looked on her. Jeremy pressed his forehead against hers and kissed the tip of her nose.

"So we are. I just didn't want to wait to do that any longer. Don't think I could have." He dropped a lingering, but less hungry, kiss to her lips, and then released her butt before he took a scooted back.

Everything slammed into him during that kiss, like something he couldn't possibly deny or run from. They might not get a happily ever after, but they weren't going to get anywhere if he didn't do the one thing that could help them both in the long run. He needed to take the DEA job and get their relationship moving. She was the one, it was time to accept what his heart had been saying for weeks. That meant doing this if he didn't want to let her slip through his fingers.

"Are you ready to go surfing now?" Bridget smiled and leaned away from him, preventing him from kissing her again.

"Would you hate me if I bailed? I can find my own way back to L.A., and there's something I need to take care of. Something that can't wait, even if it's a Saturday."

Her eyes narrowed at him, as she cocked her head to the side. Bridget shook her head, still looking at him quizzically. "Don't think I'm not going to ask what this is about later – giving me a kiss like that and then running off. The nerve."

He kissed her again quickly and then took off towards the rental shack with his board in hand.

***

Jeremy's foot was tapping almost as quickly as his heart was thumping in his chest. Three in the afternoon on a Saturday, and he was sitting across from the director of the Los Angeles DEA unit. Not what he would have ever foreseen himself doing so if he'd ever been asked.

Getting Juarez to come pick him up from the beach had been one awful explanation after the other. He'd had to explain not only the DEA's offer, but what he'd been doing down there in the first place.

However, unlike Chase, Juarez had been completely supportive of him getting his ass both into the DEA and settling down with a nice lady. He'd been so much like the father he'd always wanted. Jeremy had choked up a little in the car when Juarez had told him how proud of him he was. That breaking the rules wasn't a bad thing, but to try to not do it again, or they'd have to get a new nickname for him.

A woman walked in while he was thinking about the kiss he and Bridget shared at the beach. Her hair was impeccably pulled back, and she was wearing a gray suit seemed to be made specially for her. Despite its lack of form, it fit her perfectly. She smiled at him and he was shocked to see the smile reaching her hazel eyes.

"Very nice to meet you, Mr. Trellins. I had begun to think we were going to have our offer rejected. My name is Christy Malone. I'm the one who went to see your captain. Thank you for coming in."

Jeremy could almost feel the sweat building and dripping off his body as he did his best to shake her hands with some amount of impressive grip.

"Thank you for seeing me on a Saturday, Ma'am."

"Nonsense, the DEA works 24/7 . It's no different than the police and I was happy to come in when I heard you had requested a meeting. I do hope this will be a positive outcome for us both."

He nodded and wrung his hands together across his lap as he watched her sit down. "Yes, Ma'am. I wanted to apologize for taking so long to think about things, and to tell you how honored I am that you came to me."

"Yes, about that, are you comfortable with me asking just what delayed your decision for approximately two months?"

He sucked in air through his nose and slowly blew it out as he tried to decide which honest answer was the best to give. "A woman, Ma'am. I met someone I'm very fond of, and well, she's about to be a member of the LAPD. I didn't want to make a rash decision and come here without properly thinking my options out. I love catching the drug lords, there is a certain satisfaction in it, but I love all my work with the police as well. The decision needed to be properly thought out."

She raised a perfectly manicured blonde eyebrow at him. "You say you're involved with a co-member of the force?"

He almost puked in his mouth. "No, Ma'am. We met prior to her joining. We put an end to it once we realized she was a recruit. To be honest, Ma'am, neither of us are comfortable being without the other. It was one of the perks that drew me to accepting the job."

"I see. But you are quite certain this line of work is what appeals to you, and not the promise of a social life?"

Jeremy felt like he was going to be physically ill. The one time he'd strayed from protocol, it had landed him in so much hot water. He was surprised he hadn't run home to Montgomery yet. His eyes were fixed on Agent Malone's as he spoke.

"I'm positive. I spent time thinking this decision through because I was uncertain I would like the monotony of drug wars, dealers and addicts. I like helping the smaller crime units out as well, but in the end, drugs are my specialty. Nothing feels better than taking them out before someone loses a brother, a husband or a son to drugs. I was afraid to lose everything I'd built with the LAPD. I can't explain it, but the woman helped me to realize there was more out there than just living my job."

Agent Malone nodded her head. "Well then, if you're certain," she reached a hand over the desk and he took it, shaking it once more. "Welcome to the DEA, Mr. Trellins. Please come back on Monday to fill out the needed paperwork and speak with your captain. You may have until January second to transition out of the LAPD." She stood up and walked from behind the desk and made her way to the door, but stopped just as she stood under the doorframe.

175

"I'm pleased to have you working for me, Mr. Trellins, or should I say, Agent Trellins."

A part of him, on the inside of course, took pleasure in the way she called him Agent Trellins. He hadn't been lying to her. Bridget had helped him realize there was something beyond the LAPD. He didn't doubt his decision. She was just the icing on the cake.

It was unexplainable, but he somehow knew Bridget wouldn't get upset with the long hours he would have to put in. She'd likely understand and quite possibly even want to help. They needed to take things slow, see where they headed. Jeremy had no doubt in his mind that one day he would stand before her and go down on one knee with a diamond ring in his hand.

"Umm, Mr. Trellins?"

He turned and saw the female agent that had escorted him in standing at the door. "Yes?"

"Is there anything else we can do for you today? Or are you ready for me to see you out? Protocol, you're not an agent yet, so we can't have you wandering without me."

He could have kicked himself. Of course, they wouldn't want him to remain seated in the director's office when she had gone home for the day. He mumbled an apology and allowed her to lead him out.

"Sweet Jesus, O'Casey," Santana grunted as Bridget successfully slammed her elbow into his stomach and wrapped her ankle around his right leg, dropping him to the dirty blue work out mat beneath them.

Santana tried to sit up but Bridget slammed her boot into his stomach, dropping him back down on the mat. It was probably what people would bitch about her, using excessive force, but today she didn't care. She may be being a slight bit immature and taking the anger she felt towards Jeremy out on poor Santana simply because they were sparing.

Bridget dropped to the mat again and wrapped her arm around his neck and tugged backward. She didn't let up and continued pulling his head toward her until she felt him tap her shoulder, indicating he was done. She let go of her chokehold, and for the first time, she realized how hard she was breathing.

"Let's call it quits for the day, O'Casey." Santana shook his head. "I can't figure out how you pull off that kind of power." He rubbed his neck and his stomach. "Remind me to let Juarez give you the final self defense test. I don't think I can take a second round with you."

She flushed and muttered, "I'm sorry," before stepping back into the line of recruits beside Ashley.

"Pissed off much?' Ashley asked in a joking tone.

"I still haven't gotten more than seven words from him since that kiss." She whispered back as quietly as she could to not draw attention to them.

Jeremy had given her one of the most promise-filled, lust inducing kisses of her life on Saturday and then he'd run off. She'd expected to not hear from him every day, they had never done that, but it was almost time for the Christmas break and the end of her training. She hadn't seen him in four days, and he'd barely responded to her texts since.

"Have you tried just asking why he's avoiding you?" Ashley whispered.

"Of course I did that. He said he wasn't, and that he had news. Well, I've got news for him, . I don't care what he thinks happened between us. This sure as hell set us back."

Ashley looked like she was suppressing a laugh, which slipped out after seconds in a strangled noise. "Sorry, you said set you back. You aren't capable of being that angry with him. Your eyes don't match your words and you even softened when you spoke just then. If I didn't know any better, I'd bet you're in love with him."

Bridget flinched at the words because she'd certainly been thinking all day Saturday. But then Jeremy had ruined those thoughts by being essentially missing in action for four days. Keeping his distance from her sure felt like his way of letting her know he wasn't into it anymore.

"Shut up and go show Juarez that women can be just as deadly as the men here." She pushed Ashley forward.

Bridget had meant it as a joke, but her tone was harsher than she'd intended. Ashley gave her a small smile and walked up to Juarez. They each had to spar with both trainers in order to prove they were competent in the sections skill set. She'd started with Juarez and he'd even tried to slip in a little hint that he knew she was seeing Jeremy. As of right now they'd never decided they were seeing each other, so there was nothing for Juarez to know. Which had only led to pissing her off so badly she'd done a worse number on him than on Santana. It was stunning how they appeared to not realize how easy they went on her because she was pixie like in build. It seemed Jeremy wasn't the only male idiot on the force right now.

And if she and Jeremy were seeing each other, he damn sure hadn't actually asked. Avoiding her wasn't how a boyfriend treated the person he was in a relationship with. She crossed her arms over her chest, feeling angry again despite the knowledge that she'd scored extremely high on all the tests. Ashley's words filtered back and she wanted to ignore them but the angrier she got the more she realized how much Jeremy did mean to her.

"Go get 'em!" she shouted at Ashley as her friend bent her knees and tapped the floor, tapping into the drill.

She'd fully intended on watching Ashley, but a sudden movement near the door of the gym distracted her. The person who walked in surprised her even more so. Jeremy walked in, his short chestnut brown hair looked dark from what she assumed was water. The broad, smile when they locked eyes made her want to clobber him with something. Well, the part of her that didn't want to bolt out of line and kiss him till he begged for mercy, wanted to beat his ass.

Jeremy mouthed something from across the room. She turned her chin up at him. There was no way he expected her to not be pissed off after all this time. She flinched as she caught the end of Ashley's drill. She dropped Juarez to the floor, but it was choppy and she'd had to use her arms to bring him down. Ashley, however, seemed happy with her testing, so Bridget wasn't going to bring her friend down.

Ashley's eyes landed on Jeremy's as she got back in line, and she tapped Bridget on the shoulder. "Do you see him standing there, or are you ignoring him?"

"I'm ignoring him. He doesn't get to drop off the face of the earth and then show up looking like an Adonis and not get a little ire for it. Maybe if he'd shown up looking like death warmed over, I could have assumed he was sick. He however, looks like the cat that ate the canary, which means I'm pissed at him."

Ashley laughed and nodded. "Well, there are only two more people left, so you better get over being mad at him. Or find another way out, because you sure as heck know he isn't going to let you walk past him."

She thought about everything for a moment. Jeremy looked happy, but determined a few moments ago. Would he be foolish enough to out whatever weird relationship they had to the rest of the recruits?

"I wouldn't hold your breath." Bridget said. "He's still pretending nothing is going on. Saturday must have been some sort of deal breaker. He probably realized how badly he'd broken the rules and that's why he pulled a disappearing act."

Ashley didn't get to respond. Juarez drew the class' attention, keeping Ashley from offering Bridget her opinion.

"Well then, I'm oddly happy to announce that every single one of you succeeded in executing this portion of training. Not one of you failed to get the upper hand. However, we weren't giving it our full go. That will come next week when you take the final section of self defense training. So don't get too cocky, recruits. There's still time to fail." Juarez joked, and gave them a big toothy smile to let them know he was kidding.

Bridget really had grown to like Jeremy's partner. The older cop had reminded her a lot of her father. He was good at his job, but he didn't forget to take things less seriously sometimes. Something she'd thought she'd helped Jeremy learn, but if he really had run away thinking that his time with her on Saturday had been a mistake, then there might not be anything left for them. She wouldn't give this career up, and she wouldn't ask him to. No matter how much her stomach fluttered and her heart raced every time she snuck a peek at him across the room, she would not be that girl, not when this was about making her father proud. Even if he would never really know that she was honoring him.

"Go change back into your uniform and take your lunch. Chase has some weapons training for you." Santana's grin was almost as wide as Juarez's.

She had a bad feeling they were all in for something terrible after the meal break. Cops that smiled like that in training had evil secrets. She'd learned that early on in training.

"You see lover boy over there?" Marcus asked as he walked up to them.

"Yes, I saw him, thank you and I'm trying to figure out how to avoid him. He's been an asshole the past week, and I don't feel like talking to him right now." There wasn't an ounce of believability in her words and even Marcus knew it.

"Well, seeing as how you've been so secretive, you ever consider just walking out? Not like he will risk following you."

Marcus headed for the door. She sighed and followed him. She'd expected a smart alec comment from him. It was his thing after all. What she hadn't expected was for Jeremy to reach out and wrap his hand around her forearm as she moved past him. He tugged her to him as she tried to ignore his grip and pass him.

Her body crashed into his and for the slightest section she felt liquid heat pool between her legs as her body slid against his from the force of his action. She bit her inner cheek to keep herself from moaning. Jeremy's arms wrapped around her and pulled her into his chest. His warmth radiated out over her skin and being in his arms completely stunned her. Bridget stopped fighting and simply stood there, trying to figure out what would happen next. She could feel several people staring at them and she didn't understand why he wasn't letting go; never mind why he had done it at all after his distance the past week. All she knew was if he didn't let go any shot she had at even pretending to be angry with him would vanish into thin air.

Jeremy lowered his head and she knew he was going to kiss her. Her head disobeyed her brain's shouts to pull back, and against her better judgment, she allowed her own head to tilt backward to meet his lips. When their lips touched she felt a tiny jolt of electricity course through her body. The kiss didn't deepen, it remained chaste but it still turned her to putty in his hands. Bridget's stepped back and closed her mouth, but her body felt like it was on fire.

"What are you doing?" she asked when she found the will to pull herself backward, but his arms remained around her.

Her head whipped to the side and sure enough the ten or so people still in the gym were now staring at them in earnest. Juarez smirked at her while Santana stood there a little slack-jawed, but they were all staring. She felt about as big as a germ and wanted to turn back time and stop Jeremy from deciding to out their secret.

"I took the DEA job," Jeremy said, moments later.

She heard the words but she didn't think she'd processed them. "You what?"

He laughed and she felt his body vibrate against hers from the force of his laughter.

"I accepted the offer to work for the DEA. My work here is wonderful, but I can do just as much good with them. It means I can kiss you anytime I want. If you'll let me, that is."

Honest to goodness clapping and cheers broke out behind them. As if they were in some cheesy movie, she sincerely felt like they were in one.

"Oh. My. God. Jeremy. You did this here?" As the clapping continued she felt some of the romance slip away and more of the embarrassment.

She tried to slide out of his grasp, trying to save any ounce of dignity she might have left, but she couldn't. He kissed her once more before he released her.

"Yes, I did. Although, you're right, I probably shouldn't have done it here but I couldn't wait any longer, Bridget." He turned to Juarez and Santana and gave a little wave before looking into her eyes. "Since it's the Christmas season, and one of you is my partner, how about you pretend you didn't see this and don't punish O'Casey, and by association, the entire class for a personal experience at work?"

She couldn't process anything that was happening around her except embarrassment as it settled around her like a blanket. For all her time in the limelight, it never had invaded her personal space because she wasn't a supermodel.

Part of her was screaming "he took the job" over and over as she tried to process what he'd told her. Her other half was shouting for her to run and hide. To pray that no one talked about what had just happened and to go back to their quiet blossoming affair.

"Just this once, since you're a spiffy agent and all now." Juarez gave him a mock salute.

Jeremy faced her once more. "If you don't want to cut my manhood off for publicly embarrassing you, let me take you on a date tonight. A real one. Out in public in Los Angeles, and maybe just maybe it can end up how it did the night we met."

She wasn't certain which of the urges was going to win out. They were certainly tied. She nodded her head, not trusting her voice at first.

"Ok. Yes."

He laughed. "I'm going to pretend stunned and amazed is why you're not reacting any more excited about this." Jeremy kissed her cheek. "I'll pick you up at eight and we can discuss everything then. I promise."

She nodded once more and he finally released her. She should have felt relieved, but she felt cold instead and wanted his arms around her again. Ashley's recent comment about being in love with him flashed through her mind for a second time. She wondered if it was time to tell him time to tell herself really. But something about saying it first didn't seem all that appealing, even with this rather grand gesture.

"Jeremy," he turned around and looked back at her, "you're a jerk for disappearing on me, but I'm honestly happy you did this. You're a damned good cop, and you're going to be an even better DEA agent."

He flushed a little before giving her that small side smirk of his that melted her heart every time she saw it. Jeremy then walked down the hall without another glance in her direction.

"Well, it looks like someone was a little harder to ignore than you thought." Marcus teased.

Bridget turned to look at him. Both he and Ashley had amused smiles plastered on their faces.

"Oh, shut up." She laughed after saying the words and shook her head.

Jeremy's news had taken her by storm. Granted, she'd thought quite differently about his reasons for leaving her on Saturday. Nevertheless, she was glad that he'd taken a job that would allow them to come out of the shadows. The smile on her face felt as if it was going to be permanent and any anger she felt at her own embarrassment melted away.

"O'Casey!" Juarez called her name and jogged up to them, slightly out of breath. "You keep my partner on his toes. He needs a good woman. I'll be damned if watching you kick his ass sometimes won't be quality entertainment."

10

Nothing would ever compare to these few moments. Trevor knew that as intimately as he knew his own mind. There was a rush of sensual satisfaction that accompanied each kill. There was just something about killing a police officer that got him off. He could take a guess at what. They had screwed his life up and ending theirs had just been a plan, now it was becoming an addiction.

Trevor could feel how rapidly his heart was beating, and his eyes were laser focused as they watched on the outside of the station. Ventura, they had been the cops with the second largest task force that had tracked the crew he'd run ran with down. His plans for them were special.

"Hey, Trevor, we going to sit out here all night freezing our balls off, or are we going to make a fucking move?" Carl, an explosives expert, asked as he stood beside Trevor.

"I've told you a hundred times. I want to take half the fucking building out. We can't do that until later, or we'll never make it anywhere near those doors."

Carl sighed dramatically and Trevor made a note to put a bullet in the man's head after this hit was over. He was a pain in the ass Trevor didn't need.

"I'm out of here at ten. You can set up your own fucking bombs, you son of a bitch." Carl mumbled.

A look of annoyance spread across Trevor's face upon hearing the softly spoken insult. His hand itched to grab the handgun from his pocket and end Carl's life, then and there. Instead, he bit down on his tongue until the pain whited out his vision and titled his wrist to check his watch. Thirty-nine more minutes until ten. He wondered if they could get away with going in early.

Trevor sat down on the ground, glancing at the other two men with them, Steven and Mario. It was a huge job with a small workload tonight. Ventura County had six SWAT members the night they'd finally tracked them down and Trevor was accused of killing one of them. He wanted to be certain to take at least that many down.

The plan was simple. Steven and Mario would get into a fight right outside the precinct's doors. A real fight too. If they wanted to live past tonight, they would do it properly and not hold back any punches or Trevor would let them go in the cruelest of ways. While the smaller staff of night cops dealt with that, Carl was would set up three explosives on the side of the building and smash a window to drop a fourth in. Trevor still didn't understand how dropping one wouldn't trigger it, but Carl assured him about a dozen times it would be ok.

Trevor would be the one to make it all go boom. He had an old Pontiac waiting for him three blocks down. He'd make his move as soon as Mario and Steven began. The pair would be booked for the night, and maybe suffer a little from several priors each had held against them but they'd be just fine.

Carl was on his own to get out of there once things were said and done. The fucker was a weasel. He didn't doubt the man would get away. If he didn't, well, he was annoying the shit out of Trevor anyway.

Exactly five minutes after Mario and Steven played their parts, Trevor dial the number on the burner phone he had with him and set the four beautiful devices off. It wasn't as personal as a shooting, as watching as the cops fell to their knees, but it was the best way to take down a lot of them at once. Truth be told, he was fine with that.

Just a few more minutes, and it'll be down to just you, LAPD. Just a few more minutes and nothing will protect your police from me when I come to take you all down.

He'd been saving LAPD for last. LA had been the group's last location when they'd been caught. He wanted the last bullet he fired to go into the head of the cop that had arrested him– Jimmy O'Casey.

The sound of a small chime going off caught his attention. He whipped his head around and snarled as he saw Carl turning off his fucking watch alarm.

Trevor's right hand flew backwards and slammed into the man's face.

"Are you fucking kidding me? A god damn watch alarm? Why not tell them where the fuck we are?" he barked in a low whisper.

Mario snickered. Jeremy turned and glared at the heavyset Italian man and Mario looked at the ground. Trevor's own heartbeat sped up just a notch as he realized what the alarm meant.

Ten o'clock, time to begin.

He stood up slowly, decisively, and looked at the three men standing beside him. "This is our second to last hit. The smallest group with the biggest bang. Do not get us all caught. Do your parts properly and after we take down the LA cops of my choosing, we'll all have comfy new identities and be on our way separately to new states."

Carl nodded and tugged the black hoodie over his head and walked off of the side street first. He was going to make a circle around the police station, well, as much of a circle as he could make before running into the 101 freeway, and just look first. Carl looked

197

like a man out for a walk on a nice December night. Once done with checking his perimeter, he'd make a run for it.

Mario and Steven grinned. They high-fived each other like a pair of children and headed up Glacier Alley towards Ralston and the station.

Trevor just stood there, relishing in the rush of excitement pumping through his body. His breathing grew ragged and he could feel every fiber of his body lusting after the kill. But he had a part to play as well and that meant waiting a few minutes before he could walk down to Walker Street. From there, he'd head on and then over to Saratoga Avenue where his nice little beater car and burner phone waited.

He counted the seconds in his head, his eyes dancing back and forth making sure no one could see him, his ears painfully straining to hear if he could make out any sort of indication that the fight had begun. No sound of any sort reached his ears, however. He cursed and clenched his fists – this could be the plans downfall. If he didn't know when to start walking, he could mess the timing up.

"Idiot." Trevor growled in frustration.

He punched the nearest mailbox and his face went white as the stupidity of the action registered. Quickly, he whipped his head around to make sure that no one had seen or heard him. Trevor sucked in a lungful of air through his nose and faced the opposite side of the street. He forced himself to whistle, a habit he hated in others, but found that it calmed him down immensely.

There was no sign of the fight that was supposed to be going on came to him. He looked down at his watch as he turned onto Walker Street. In five minutes, everything was going to get very loud either way.

Trevor wished he could hear some sign of what was going on, or that they'd thought of a clever way for Carl to call or text without compromising himself. Carl had squealed like a pig when they'd caught him last time and since Trevor's prints had been on the gun, and it was registered to him in the first place, the cops had believed he'd been alone. Trevor didn't doubt Carl would do the same if caught again, so each one of them making it out had been the most important thing. Now that Carl was pissing him off, if the man was too dumb to get away from his own bombs, that was his fault. The teal green Sunbird came into view as it sat beneath the streetlight Trevor had parked it under several hours earlier. His whistling stopped as the grin of satisfaction spread across his face.

"Three more minutes. I walk fast." he said to absolutely no one at all as he pulled open the door and slid into the dirty car. "Three more minutes."

His left hand thrummed on the wheel as he dug through the center console and pulled out the burner phone. His eyes glazed over as a fantasy full of shocked screams and pain played out inside his head. He laughed, imagining the chaotic scene, the police unaware of what was going on. Ventura County had money, and that's what made this victory so much sweeter. The cops were too focused on drug deals and other crimes. For whatever reason, very few people were dumb enough to try and bomb a police department.

"And very few people have the drive I have." He suspected the sentence was false, very few parolees ever pulled off what he'd done in the last three months.

Beep, beep. Beep, beep. Beep, beep.

The cell phone's alarm went off, 10:10. The magic number. Trevor pushed the fantasy aside and dragged his finger across the device in the sequence Carl had shown him.

For a second, nothing happened. Trevor wondered if he'd been played, or if something had gone wrong. Then, a sound so loud that it hurt his ears, rang out. In the distance, a mushroom cloud of smoke billowed into the air. The ground beneath him shook from the force of the explosion, even though Carl had made some pretty mild bombs, not much stronger than a home made pipe bomb. A shred of terror consumed him momentarily worrying that five blocks had been stupidly close.

People ran out of several houses and businesses that lined the street. He grew worried again about getting caught. Forcing one deep breath and then another, he put the key in the ignition. He wouldn't drive toward Dowell Street; he wouldn't get to see the perfection of his team's plan. He would get out of the area unscathed, nonetheless. No one would ever know he'd been there in the first place. He relished the thought of seeing the destruction his team had caused on the morning news though.

"Yes, I certainly will see it then."

His hands gripped the wheel and slammed the gear stick into place. Trevor pulled out of his parking spot, smiling as he took in the ensuing chaos that surrounded him.

"Jimmy O'Casey, I'm coming for you." There were five Jimmy O'Casey's on the force in southern California, his research hadn't been deep, but one of them just had to be his man.

11

Jeremy gently stroked his fingers over Bridget's exposed arm. She squealed and pulled away from him.

"How many times do I have to tell you that tickles, Trellins?"

Her tone was playful as she punched his arm. The blanket slipped downward, exposing her body to him. Desire began to course through his veins.

He chuckled despite the lust forming within him. "Well, maybe I like tickling you."

She snorted, "well, maybe I don't feel like having morning sex with you."

Bridget sounded like a petulant child and he laughed. She tried to stand up out of the bed, but he wrapped his arms around her from behind and tugged her backward once more. He placed several kisses along the curve of her neck and whispered into her ear.

"You know, you're going to need to defend yourself better than that out on the streets."

A second later, her elbow slammed into his gut and knocked the wind out of him. She twisted her head and looked over her shoulder at him, grinning so hard at him he wondered if her smile ever broke cameras when she was modeling.

"I was unaware you were a danger."

Her voice dropped an octave and the husky tone of it sent a wave of blood rushing to his dick. Three days had passed since he'd publically staked his claim on her in the training room like a lovesick fool and they'd been inseparable since that night. He'd taken her on a proper date to McCormick's, where to his shock, she ordered the fish and not the steak. He'd spent most of the last two days keeping her distracted from the world outside.

The Ventura County Police Department had been hit the night they'd had dinner together. They'd been so intently focused on one another, they hadn't heard the news of about it until the next morning when they'd been getting ready – her for the academy, and him just to enjoy some R&R. Captain had let him go two weeks early in light of the Bridget situation.

She'd bottomed out. He'd never seen someone hit the floor so quickly, and the tears. God the tears. No one should ever experience that much grief in a lifetime, let alone a moment. Unfortunately, he knew so many people in life did.

However, that moment had brought them closer together than anything else they'd experienced in more ways than one. Taking care of her, easing her through the pain and sadness, had triggered something in him. He wanted to be the one to take care of her for the rest of their lives. He wasn't certain he was completely in love with her, but he was falling in love damn fast with her, and there was nothing he would change about it. Except maybe the rocky slope in the beginning.

Bridget O'Casey was his perfect other half. She understood his need to put work first, and he had a feeling she might do so in the future as well. She was compassionate, had self-defense and shooting skills that rivaled the best of the guys on the force, loved to pig out while watching a good game– he'd learned that last night during a hockey match on pay-per-view– and she was absolutely stunning. He wanted to keep waking up next to her tousled, dark, short hair and beautiful eyes for as long as she'd let him.

"I think you owe me a shooting competition, Jeremy."

He wrapped his arms around her again. This time, she leaned against him.

"Don't you think it would give you an unfair advantage over the other recruits if you trained with your ex-cop boyfriend?" He playfully dragged his fingers down her back, loving the way she shivered and arched away from him.

"Don't you think it's not fair that you're afraid to let your girlfriend beat you?" She turned her head and pressed her lips to his. It was a gentle kiss but still enough to make his cock twitch.

"Mmm, you know what I think is unfair?" He suckled the sweet spot where her graceful neck met her shoulders. "That you blatantly teased me about morning sex, are parading around naked and then kiss me like that." He trailed his right hand down her bare stomach before settling it between her legs.

"Something tells me –" she paused as he dragged three fingers over her swollen clit, "-that you will be able to convince me otherwise."

She exhaled a breath and he felt her shift her body against his and her legs parted.

"That's what I like to hear." He slipped a finger inside of her, and moved it in and out in a steady pace as he circled her clit with his index finger while he spoke.

Bridget's breathing hitched and a moan came from her slightly parted lips. Jeremy swore he saw stars as his cock hardened and pressed against her back. He slid a second finger inside of her and quickened how they alternated and thrust within her wet heat. Her hips moved forward instinctively, riding his fingers.

He loved the way she gave in to him with such abandonment, and didn't limit herself or hide from him this way. He began to scissor his fingers within her, causing her to cry out. A small smirk spread across his lips at the knowledge he was satisfying her. Her hips were thrusting faster now, jerking back and forth against him. A mewl of disappointment escaped her as he pulled his two fingers out of her.

"That was unfair." she said through panted breaths.

He let go of her completely and rolled over her body, stopping with his body just above hers, the tip of his cock teasing her entrance. Jeremy rolled further off of her and stood up, grabbing a condom from the dresser drawer he had learned she kept them in. Sheathing himself, he leaned over her once more, putting his arms on either side of her head, and slowly ground his hips against her. His erection swept over her with the briefest of touches and he had to focus to not growl his own approval at the same time as she whimpered beneath him.

"Maybe it was because I would rather have you come with me inside of you." Bridget looked up at him, desire lurking in her eyes. He wrapped his fingers around his aching cock and guided himself into her, burying himself to the hilt. "Jesus, you feel so perfect every fucking time, Bridget." Every word was punctuated by a thrust of his dick.

He was the one panting out breaths now as he forced his body to slowly thrust in and out of her, building up their need. Her hands dragged down his back, her nails scoured across his skin and his body twitched at the connection. He loved when she did that.

She lifted her legs, crossed her ankles around his ass and tugged him downward, pushing him deeper into her body.

She tilted her head up and pressed her mouth to his. All thoughts fled his mind as her tongue slipped into his mouth. She bucked as he slid into her body deeper and her hips began to rock faster against his. He let her take the lead, thrusting into her with reckless abandonment. All he could feel was her core wrapped around him, squeezing him. It was sheer blissful torture.

Their bodies were slick with sweat when they pressed and slapped together as controlled thrusts became wild and needy. He couldn't be certain who was groaning louder or moving faster. It felt as if what one did, the other did. His body tightened with every stroke of their bodies and tongues.

He felt it as her orgasm began, the way her body clenched around his cock, the way it quivered as tiny jolts of her orgasm began. He could feel her every part of it and it made his own body rush closer and closer to an orgasm. She cried out into his mouth, as her hips bucked up one last time and her body shook with pleasure. Her hands dug into his shoulders and her body spasmed and tightened around him. That was all it took.

His own release slammed into him without warning. It was the best damn thing he'd ever felt to come at the same time as her body was still experiencing the side effects of her own pleasure.

Jeremy's vision was hazy and he allowed himself to just lie there and savor the moment. Every muscle in his body felt drained, the perfect feeling after making love. He pulled out of her, moments later, and rolled gently over her body to lay on his back.

"That, may have been the best sex I've ever had." he said.

"I cannot disagree with that statement."

They lay there in silence, breathing deep for several minutes. He grabbed her hand and brought it to his mouth. Sensually, he placed a kiss to the top of it. Entwining his fingers with hers, he turned to look at her. She looked damned sexy with her hair plastered to her face. Jeremy laughed abruptly at the fact that he found her, slick with sweat, sexy as hell.

"You're pretty amazing, Bridget O'Casey." The words were out before he knew he was even thinking them.

Bridget smiled at him, not the big boisterous smile he was used to seeing, but a shy stripe of one across her face. A dull flush of color spread across her cheeks. He had a feeling he had just come very close to making her blush as the light pink colored her face.

"You're something pretty special yourself, Jeremy Trellins." She closed her eyes for a few long seconds before opening them once more. "I know you didn't take the DEA job for me, for us, but I won't lie to you and pretend like I'm not overjoyed that you did. Now that I'm over the shock of it."

Jeremy slid off the bed and made his way to the bathroom to quickly discard the condom. He returned to bed several seconds later. Bridget pressed her head against his chest as he lay back down and he wrapped his arms around her.

" I'm quite glad I did, too. I may be a little scarce during training. In fact, I know I will be. Seeing you between now and then will be tough at best. I didn't want to tell you, to assume we'd be seeing one another in another few weeks, but there's one week till Christmas, and two until the New Year. I thought it was a fairly safe bet."

She kissed his lips gently and then went back to laying her head back against his chest. "I kind of expected as much. You just have to promise that when you're done, we can make up for all the missed opportunities – however many or long it takes."

He chuckled and felt her face tug into a smile against his chest. "I promise Bridget O'Casey. The way I feel now, I could happily make it up to you for a lifetime."

She sat up and looked at him. The playfulness was gone from her face, but she didn't look serious either, a little spooked perhaps.

"Did you just imply that you were in love with me?"

He laughed. "I think I implied I was falling in love with you, yes." He leaned over and gave her a peck this time. "Pretty damn fast, I might add."

She smiled at him. "I would say three months is fairly standard. But in case you were wondering, I'm pretty close to being done falling myself."

He smirked, unintentionally. "Now that is something mighty fine to hear." he said, his southern accent thickening as he spoke because he knew how it affected her. "That first night when you pulled away from me, I was a bit worried it was one-sided."

"I was just nervous about starting at the academy. Besides, can you imagine how weird it would have been in the morning if one of us happened to say where work was, or something to that extent?"

He laughed and she did as well. They both knew just how awkward things really would have been since they had a pretty heavy dose of awkward at the station.

"It certainly would have been. Now, about that shooting competition?"

"Yes? Sure you're not afraid of being taken down by a slip of a woman?"

He grinned and shook his head. "I was thinking we could hold off and raise the stakes. What do you say to a little action during your simulation final? I think I could convince Danvers to let me in, other officers have stepped in before to make things a little harder."

She laughed. "I knew it. You're chicken."

He gasped. "Southern men are never chicken."

"Well, the one next to me in this bed sure is."

She began to make clucking noises. Jeremy started tickling her. She rolled around the bed, gasping for breath, helplessly clawing at him through her laughter.

"Say mercy, or I bet you'll pee yourself." He was laughing so hard the words were difficult to get out.

"Mercy! Mercy!" she shouted, and when he stopped she kept rolling fitfully around the bed for a minute, like she had no idea he wasn't touching her anymore.

"Oh, there's going to be payback for that, mister." She stood up out of bed. "Come on, let's go. You're not getting out of it now."

He lay back, partially sitting up and smirked at her. "I think I can handle you. I'm fairly certain that was a victory for me."

She snorted and walked into the bathroom. "Ten minutes. Be ready to have your ass kicked."

"Congratulations, you've just finished the beginning of the end. For those of you on track, you have my respect. For those of you not, you still have four days to get those tests and qualifications passed. You're not excused just yet, but a test score isn't going to magically make all your other non-qual scores work. So get to it and come see me to schedule extra test times if the class one's don't work. The rest of this week is going to be a ton of reviews, so be ready to impress me." Chase said, and smiled at them, the first real smile Bridget had seen from him since they had begun at training so many weeks ago.

"So, how's it feel to be top of our class, miss perfect?" Marcus asked as they walked out of the classroom.

She flushed. Bridget was proud of herself, though she felt guilty about doing so well when Ashley and Marcus weren't. Plus, she had essentially abandoned them since she and Jeremy had moved things to an official level.

"It feels nice. I'm sorry I haven't been around to help out more. Or hang out." She looked at the ground as Ashley gave a lighthearted laugh.

"I think spending time in bed with a sexy soon-to-be federal agent is reason enough to leave us common folk behind."

"Ashley, I don't think there's a damned thing common about you," Marcus teased as they got off the elevator and walked through the intake floor behind the cop who escorted them today.

"Anyone else find it odd that we are still walking around the precinct with a uniform?" she asked.

Marcus shrugged. She barely caught it out of the corner of her eye.

217

"Only because there's like three hundred cops working here. I feel like we meet a new one everyday, and then poof, someone else has babysitting duty." Ashley laughed.

The cop escorting them laughed and then another shouted something.

"Another one? Are you fucking serious? How has no one caught these fuckers?"

Bridget froze. *Another one what?* Someone answered her mental thought before she even vocalized it.

"If they don't catch the shooters soon, there's going to be a statewide panic."

Bridget swallowed. It felt like she had swallowed hundreds of shards of glass. Her head whipped around to see the two male cops standing by the water cooler like it really was an office gossip spot.

"What do you mean another one? Did they attack more cops?" She had turned around and was walking toward them as she asked.

For a moment, she didn't think they were going to answer. One of them gave her a once over and then a confused look, as if there was no way a recruit was talking to him. The other looked at her and shook his head.

"Down in Santa Cruz. Media hasn't gotten there yet, but it sounded like it was a much lower key hit than the bombings a few days back."

"But there was definitely another attack? On police?"

She could hear the panicked edge in her voice as she spoke but she didn't care. With every attack that happened she grew more and more concerned of two things. She wondered if the Los Angeles Police Department was somewhere on the hit list. If there was a chance the people that shot her father outside the cop hangout were a part of this.

"Absolutely. These freaks have some expert skills because they're getting away with what they're doing. Well, they were. I don't think they stand a chance from here on out. Counties are onto them now, and they won't get away with another one."

It felt as if something possessed her. One minute, she'd been calmly walking out the door. The next, she'd walked away from her escort, and now she was literally running through the building toward Captain Danvers office. They had only been shown it once, but she knew where it was because of her father's time on the force.

"O'Casey, stop right there!" Whoever had been escorting them must have been the one that shouted.

"O'Casey. God damn it, O'Casey, stop!" Someone grabbed her wrist, and jerked her entire body causing her to stumble as her knees buckled. "Get up. Fuck, I can't believe I'm going through this with my best recruit."

Her eyes widened as she realized Chase had been the one to grab her. He must have been on his way up and had seen her running like an idiot. She didn't struggle against him as he helped her to her feet. Her good sense a`nd logic slowly returned.

"What the fuck was you thinking? You damn well know you're to be in the company of an officer the entire time. The last fucking week, and you choose to break the rules!?" Chase's voice was stern and laced with disappointment.

For a split second, she felt bad about what she'd done.

"I have to know what happened today. My father–"

"Was shot a few months back. We all know about it. More than half of us were at his ceremony. That doesn't explain why you freaked out and ran away like that."

"I have to know what happened. What if these are the people that killed my father? You didn't catch them."

"No, we didn't. It was a he though, not a them. You know this. Shake it off, O'Casey. You can't do this shit. You're a danger if you keep losing control like this."

He tugged her towards the captain's office. She caught sight of Marcus and Ashley. They frowned as she was led in the other direction. Shame slowly started to trickle into her subconscious. She'd bolted through a police station, uncaring of the consequences.

"You're taking me to the captain anyway, aren't you?"

Chase's voice seemed legitimately sad as he nodded. "There's no other choice. Full house out there, and they all saw you do it."

Her cheeks grew warm. Several tears blurred her vision. She didn't trust herself to say anything and nodded instead. *What's Jeremy going to think when he hears about this latest stunt?* She didn't know why she thought he would disapprove, probably because she'd broken two codes of conduct in just as many seconds.

With her eyes downcast, she walked alongside Chase to the next floor. He knocked on the door leading to Captain Danvers' office. When Chase knocked Danvers waved them in without looking up from the papers on his desk.

"Sir, I know you must be busy now. We've a little disciplinary situation you need to know about."

Danvers looked up, his eyes focused on Bridget. "Bridget – –Miss O'Casey, whatever could you have done? Your dad was older than me, but I still know you grew up coming around here after school. Shit, I remember your high school graduation, we all went."

She flinched at the knowledge that she'd managed to disappoint one of her father's friends. They'd never been partners, but they'd served together almost twenty years ago. Danvers was nearing retirement now, but he'd been young when he started. Her father had him over for dinner a lot when she was growing up.

"O'Casey decided she was going to take a little jog through the station without an escort." The tone of Chase's voice was hard, though he wasn't that angry about what she'd done.

Danvers sighed. For a moment, Bridget wanted to crawl into a hole and vanish. "What brought this on?"

"The shooting. The one in Santa Cruz, sir. I wanted to know more about it. I can't shake the feeling my father was killed by the same people." Her voice trembled slightly as she spoke when she brought up her father and she silently cursed herself for looking like a child.

"And this made you run through the building?" Danvers sounded confused and it just helped to emphasize how stupid her choice had been.

She nodded. "Yes, sir. It was impulsive. I know that, but I don't know what happened. These shootings, they're taking a toll on me. I don't want to admit that, but I have to."

Chase's face softened as he looked at her. "They're concerning to us all. However, I can assure you there is no attachment to your father's murder. While we didn't catch the shooter, the description fits someone he put into the drunken tank a few years back. Found out the guy was carrying, and when he was released, he went after your father. One person and the witnesses have all verified that. This is a group of people. So far, we don't have any motive, since there seems to be no rhyme or reason behind the killings."

She said nothing, only stared at him.

"This behavior is unacceptable. Before you are to complete your course, you will have an evaluation to see if you are able to proceed. It can be scheduled after the actual testing, as I'm certain this is nothing more than a little residual worry. But it will happen before we determine if you are one of the newest of LA's finest."

She nodded. "Thank you, Sir. I'm sorry. But I have to know, what happened in Santa Cruz?"

Danvers was the one to shake his head this time, he shook it no. "That's not information you're able to have access too. I don't even know how much I've been given. Do not question it me again, or there will be a lot more than a psych evaluation and a lot less possibility you'll walk out of that training room as a cop."

Bridget swallowed past the lump in her throat, unsure of what to say or do. She wasn't certain which she wanted to do more; feign an apology or shout at him? In the end, she did neither.

"I understand."

"Alright then. Chase, walk her out. And Bridget? Don't get in Jeremy's way this week. I've asked him to come in and look at some of the reports during a meeting. He shouldn't be here long, but he was a

225

damn good cop, and I want him in on the meeting to see if he can spot an angle."

She nodded.

"All right, let's go, O'Casey."

She did her best to hold back a sigh. If Jeremy was coming in to consult, then that meant the LAPD was going to be working on this. Someone was hunting them for reasons unknown to them, which meant all the counties were also going to work together to solve this, once and for all.

Jeremy turned his head and looked at the clock. They'd been sitting in the gigantic press conference room for the better part of four hours. For some reason, it made his skin crawl. It had only been a little over a week since he'd put his new uniform on. Being there as a consultant with no actual power to do anything unnerved him.

"We've gone over everything we've had. We have reason to believe that the Ventura attack is indeed a part of the same game plan. There's no way to tell for certain. That attack was on a grander scale, but the time frame fits that of the other shootings. Once again, something was done right under our noses. The bullets do not match from any of the shootings either. We've hit every damned dead end you can think of and until we get a step closer to a conclusion, no one leaves this room," Captain Marjket, captain of the Ventura Police Department, said as she paced around the room.

Jeremy understood her worry. Her department had taken a hit far more severe than any of the others to date. Santa Barbara lost two men, San Diego lost three along with and a female prison guard. Santa Cruz had fifteen causalities, but thankfully, no deaths. Ventura lost an entire section of their building, eleven officers were dead and seven more were in the hospital.

He scratched a spot just above his eye and sighed. They'd been over everything, from the guns and bullets to the time of the shooting. They'd tried to take into account how many different directions of open fire occurred to pinpoint how many assholes they were dealing with. After all of it, the only thing Jeremy was certain of was that whoever was behind this, they were smart and had what it took to get away with this and leave people from six districts were twiddling their fucking thumbs.

Every single shooting utilized bullets that were a match to a registered gun whose owner was dead. Dead ends. All had different numbers of supposed shooters, from as many as eight in Santa Barbara to only three in Santa Cruz earlier in the day – well yesterday based on the time. There didn't appear to be any rhyme or reason for the men and women hit, with the exception of the prison guard in San Diego, she had been taken from her home and not the station. A note had been left behind, printed from a computer that left no doubt that she was apart of this mess.

Jeremy had a damn good feeling it was a personal strike, all of it. The body of the guard they'd found was his only true clue. She'd been tortured prior to her death according to the autopsy. It seemed as if the killer had a specific reason to hate her.

"Has anyone considered the possibility of a grudge match?" He spoke up out of the blue, and three captain's heads whipped towards him – consultants typically didn't speak out in meetings.

"Of course, we'd be fools not to after a string of them not to consider that option," said Marjket said.

"Yes, but has anyone taken the time to process which of the guards from Cheryl's people had been let out recently? She's your one mistake. Everything else has been cold and distant. Her death was deliberate, passionate. You find someone you can link directly to her, and you'll have at least one of your shooters."

"We've tried that, Trellins. Well, not us specifically at the LAPD, but the SDPD pulled files immediately. She'd worked with so many felons over the course of her entire career. Nothing coincided with a recent release. Nothing more than a few drunks and strung out druggies. They wouldn't have the firepower or really the edge to do what was done to her," Danvers said, sighing as he dragged his hands over his eyes.

"We aren't getting anywhere. We don't even know for certain where else this group will hit. We have confirmation this isn't happening in other states, so this is not an uprising of sorts. We've seen a pattern that seems to point to repeat attacks not being an issue. Which, if we start at Santa Barbara and work our way south to San Diego, that still leaves San Bernardino, Orange County, and Los Angeles as counties not yet targeted," Captain James, captain of the Santa Barbara Police Department, stated.

"Which leaves them vulnerable," added the chief from Orange County. "Vulnerable, and with officers and family members sitting around wondering and worrying when they might be next. We need to catch whoever this is and we need to catch them before they take anyone else down."

The cacophony of voices murmuring in agreement around the room sounded like a roar of thunder. Jeremy looked around and took in the faces of almost one hundred and fifty people in the room. There were too many of them. Too many voices battling to be heard and it was part of the reason why they'd been here four hours and only managed to put together a small piece of the information that they didn't know.

He could technically get up and leave anytime he wanted since he wasn't on payroll anymore. He was a consultant, here to do nothing more than volunteer information. He had no badge, no gun, nothing tying him to the chair. Except how badly his blood boiled that someone or some group of people were targeting the law enforcement agencies in Southern California. Every time someone had gone down each and every police officer in the country would have felt the pain of losing someone on the force to such brutal killings. He had wanted to believe in that. Because in his mind, there was a chance these people were dirty cops pulling off the jobs.

"What about the possibility of insiders?" He voiced his internal question, prepared for what would come next. Jeremy was met with the curses and hisses he thought he would so he stood up and raised his hands in a sign of defense. "Just give me a second

231

here. Think about it as a possibility before you castrate me. Trained officers would have access to multiple weapons belonging to dead people. Trained officers would know how to pull off hits without getting attacked. And whether you want to suck down the bitter taste in your mouth and admit it or not, everyone has dirty cops. They're filthy parasites, and they hide somewhere in every department, in every county."

The room didn't erupt as he'd expected it too. A few people scoffed at the idea, but no one jumped down his throat again to disprove his theory. This should have made him feel ecstatic. The fact that cops could be killing their own took away any feeling of glory he had at creating a viable explanation.

"If only there was a way to sniff them out," Captain James said, his face etched with annoyance. "For now, we keep thinking. Thank you– Trellins, was it? Please sit back down as we are not done here."

His mind tried to turn over several different possibilities as he tuned out more of the worthless babble occurring throughout the room once he'd sat back down. The trick was to find out what the counties had in common–what criminals and what crime statistics–anything that could paint a better picture. It pissed him the fuck off that he couldn't think of anything.

Jeremy riffled through the gigantic stack of stapled papers in front of him that held all the evidence they currently had. Sitting here, talking and turning pages, wasn't going to do anything.

"Time to call your families, folks. This is going to be a long night."

He wasn't certain who had said it, but he was pretty certain every person in the room groaned. None of them loved nights like this, not even him. He narrowed his eyes at the paper and sat up a little straighter in his chair. He'd done things like this with Danvers before. If they gave power to the biggest department, they weren't getting out of here until they had a suspect, a target, and a date for what might be the next attack.

"Son of a bitch!"

Without thinking, Trevor threw his cell phone across the room. He'd secured the needed minimum wage job at a Chipotle to keep his parole officer off his back. He'd been waiting throughout that shift to find out where the final Jimmy O'Casey on the list lived. Sadly, his phone had died on his shift, and there were no chargers on the bus. He didn't like excess connection with his boys, safer for everyone involved that way, so he had to wait. But, he wasn't a tech guru, he didn't have the smarts to things on his own so he needed his team.

He'd been practically salivating at the idea of sending his guy, Mikey, into snatching the ex-cop so

234

he could torture him. Getting back to his tiny one bedroom apartment in Escondido, he hadn't expected to find that the fucker already dead.

His hands clenched. His knuckles whitened by the second from clenching so hard after launching the phone. "That son of bitch wasn't allowed to up and die on his own terms."

Huffing, he stalked over and picked up the phone up off the floor and continued to read the rest of the article on the cop's death. As he did a slow smile spread across his lips.

"Well, well, well. At least if I couldn't take him down the way I wanted to, it's nice to know that someone did. I wonder how often these idiots fail to catch killers."

He let the thought wash over him. He'd been planning his revenge for four hundred days. He'd made sure each and every gun was essentially unmarked, belonging to a dead person that he'd gotten on the black market, ensuring their safety. He'd taken painstaking time to ensure each gun was disposed of so it couldn't accidentally be used again.

Each group had different shooters, with the exception of himself. If one person could get away with shooting a cop in plain sight, then he and his boys had nothing to worry about.

He dragged a hand over the screen and continued to smile. Jimmy O'Casey had a very hot daughter. He felt the swell of his dick and shifted his pants. He hadn't gotten hard thinking about anything other than killing cops in months. Feeling something by looking at a photo was a shock, but he wasn't about to ignore it – not completely.

He pushed the number to reach Mikey and waited impatiently as it rang.

"Do we have a hit tonight? I thought you wanted to wait a day or so?" Mikey's voice sounded a little panicked.

"It's ok, we're actually going to push this back a little. How are your hacking skills?"

He could practically see the grin spreading over his oldest accomplice's face in his tone of voice. Mikey had been the brightest star in their group back in the day. He'd been the only one of them in school and he'd been a fucking genius.

"Better than ever. What's that got to do with anything?"

"I need you to check up on someone. Someone I want to add to the list of cops I want to take down at the LAPD."

"We had a list? I thought that Cheryl bitch was the only one you specifically wanted other than O'Casey?"

"It seems our dear pal has met his end, but has a hot as Hell daughter, I want her. Bridget O'Casey, so says the article I found on her dad. She's a model. Track her down. Find out where she is. If she's back in the Los Angeles area, she's mine."

Mikey was quiet. For a moment Trevor thought he lost him, but then an impressed whistle came through the phone several seconds later.

"Damn, O'Casey made a beautiful kid."

"That he did," Trevor reached down and stroked himself through his pants, feeling excited as he thought about Bridget O'Casey. "So, you're going to

237

find her. You've got till this evening. I don't want to lose all the fear we've built. I want this last attack to happen this week. I just want to include a little extra fun. A side dish to the main course.

Mikey chuckled. "Give me ten minutes, and I can have anything you want on her."

"Good. You've now set a timeline for yourself." Trevor disconnected the call and tossed the cheap smartphone onto the bed, and sat down on the edge. "Five hundred and ninety-seven days in jail, and it's finally almost over."

His voice was low as he slid his pants off and grabbed himself and slowly stroked his aching cock. Bridget O'Casey's face was burned deep into his mind and he was never one to let a good erection go to waste.

***

Trevor smirked at the incoming text. It amazed him how talented Mikey was, and how stupid people were with their information systems. Bridget

O'Casey's address was now in his hands, Complete with directions from the nearest bus stops to her front door. Which meant there was nothing that was stopping him from looking in on dear old Jimmy's baby girl.

If he was going to snatch her, which was the only plan he could think of right now, he'd need to stop by her house a few times and to look at the surroundings, not to mention learn her habits.

"So give yourself two days. See when she comes and goes, and check on the neighbors."

He released a pent-up breath. The idea of having to snatch someone else made him sweat, literally. Taking Cheryl hadn't been impossible, but doing it again was a test of skill he hadn't perfected.

Trevor grabbed his wallet off the desk and headed for the door, punching in the bus route information as he walked to it. Not once did his footsteps fumble along the way. His mind raced, though it was laser focused as ever on the task at hand. Getting caught tonight, or during any surveillance time, would ruin it all.

The cold didn't bother him as he waited for the bus. The bitter annoyance that he would be reporting in for a god-forsaken early morning shift at the restaurant was the only thing that bothered him.

Just keep it together. This is it. The final step before you punish everyone who put you away for no reason. His voice buzzed in his mind as he stepped onto the bus.

He rummaged through his pocket for the change and dropped his ass into a seat three rows back. According to the directions, he had twenty minutes to wait until his stop.

Trevor thrummed his fingers across his jean-clad knees. *Twenty minutes isn't so bad. Having a place in LA was a damn good idea.* He just needed to distract himself. Because right now all he could think about was sinking his hands into the short cut hair of Bridget O'Casey. He wanted to fuck her. There was really nothing that said he couldn't, or shouldn't.

"Not like they make a rule book for this shit." He hadn't realized he'd spoken out loud until he saw the man next to him giving him a look.

Trevor shrugged his shoulders and pulled out his phone. It wasn't fancy, but he could surf the Internet a bit in the meantime.

The Internet didn't help. His thoughts alternated between fucking the lovely female and slitting her throat. Something about the way blood seeped out over him, the way he could feel the pulse before it stopped, felt so much more personal. The airlock suction sound of the bus door opening snapped him out of his reverie just in time for him to jump off the bus and race off. He practically threw himself out of the bus and then stopped to take a look around.

"Son of bitch."

He'd already forgotten the next step in the directions. Grumbling, he pulled his phone back out and scanned them over before lifting his head to double check the street sign in front of him. Sucking in a deep breath to calm the anger rolling within him, he started walking.

It was a nice area really. He passed several small businesses along the way before slipping into the nice picket fence area. She lived just outside the city, and probably liked it out here. He knew he did. It was quieter, cleaner, and luckily for him, had considerably less cops wandering around unless called.

Every house was perfect. Nothing cookie cutter, the area was too old for that. Each one had a perfectly mown lawn with expertly trimmed bushes and power washed driveways. According to her online Lazy Girls page she was with American Model Management; whoever the hell they were, she was a model. He could easily see how she'd amassed the money to live out here at such a young age. If he took a second to really think about it, he'd probably be jealous.

Nothing had ever been easy for him. His family had grown up blue collar. Mom and Dad made just enough to feed him and his three brothers, but there was never anything extra to go around. No huge Christmas's or birthdays. No car when he or his brother's turned sixteen.

It had been his dad's temper that had been the problem. The man hadn't even needed to drink to take a swing at them for something. His older brother,

Travis, had protected them as long as he could. He'd joined the Marines, though, and it had left him alone to protect his two youngest brothers.

A shudder raced through him as he thought about how many beatings he had taken, many of which had been meant for his brothers. *It's a shame I can't get back at that son of a bitch now.*

The thought crossed his mind and a bitter mood passed over him. His dad had died three years ago. He'd heard about it through the lock-up grapevine. His mom had gone to visit him, but he'd told his mother to go away. Not like it really mattered that the old man was dead, but he should have pretended to be as good of son as he was pretending to be a model citizen.

"3752, 3754…" Travis quietly repeated the numbers of the houses across the street. Bridget lived in 3808, just a few houses down.

When he got to it he stopped across the street next to a blue Honda parked along the sidewalk. Trevor decided to sit down behind it and just observe from across the way. He wasn't sure how long he would have, and he wanted to memorize what the area was like at night. He'd also check it out during the day tomorrow to see which time would be the best to grab her, assuming she even stayed home during the day. She was a model, there was no information as to what she'd be doing right now, or how long she even planned on staying in the area, just that she'd returned home for her father's funeral.

A light was on in the front window. He wondered if the blinds ever opened. His cock throbbed for a moment, eager to get a glimpse of her in her own home. He lifted his hand up and bit down on the back of it to deflate the sudden rise of his desire. It worked like a charm, and he was able to focus again on watching.

Forty minutes went by. The beeping of his cell phone shocked Trevor from his seated position behind the car. Nothing had happened. Some people had walked by on her side of the sidewalk, but she hadn't come out and the light in the upper window hadn't gone out. Nor had any others turned on. If she had a dog, it hadn't barked like the others in the area twelve minutes ago. Which meant she was most likely in for the night and alone.

The quiet of the suburb was nice. It meant that he would have less trouble getting into her house because less people would be out. It did mean he would need to be quieter if she lived alone, which he thought she did as it was a one-car garage, then she would hear any intrusion. He would need to sneak into her home before she came back.

His phone beeped twice. He growled at it, like it would help silence it from dying. If his phone died, he'd miss the last bus back. Pushing himself off the cold ground, he stretched a little and started heading back towards the bus. Two more would be running before midnight. He had plenty of time, even if it was almost a forty-minute walk from the stop.

The night hadn't been a bust. It hadn't told him much, but it had confirmed a few things. She was home at night, she had no pet, and she lived alone. He would just need to get back here on the first bus in the morning to see when she went out, if she did at all.

A small smile spread across his lips. In a matter of months he'd added kidnapping, stalking, and murder to his list of crimes. It was a shame they'd never catch him to lock him up for the shit he really had committed.

14

Jeremy couldn't stop the yawn as he pulled up outside of Bridget's house. They'd been at it for almost twenty-four hours straight at the station and his head was spinning. What was worse was they weren't any closer to figuring out how many people were behind the shootings, or who any single one of the perps was. He put the car in park and stretched when he got out of the vehicle.

"I will not miss those sessions. I will not miss those sessions." He chanted it like a mantra as he slammed the car door.

A shit ton of effort had gone into a meeting that had largely gone unfulfilled. Time he could have been spent enjoying his technically new relationship with

Bridget. Instead, he'd spent it with too much coffee and creamer, and a lot of stodgy old men and uptight women.

Not that they didn't have anything to be that way about, he thought as he looked around Bridget's quiet, upscale neighborhood.

The sleepy little suburban area was quiet, as it should have been at 5:45 in the morning. The sun's golden rays were slowly peeking over the hills. For a split second, he actually missed the open plains of Alabama, and watching the sunsets and dawns there.

He wondered if Bridget would be awake. The last thing he wanted to do was to quietly sneak in and get assaulted if she had a registered weapon. She was a cops kid – she likely had one somewhere. For his own safety, he pulled out his phone and sent her a quick text asking if she was awake.

While waiting, Jeremy leaned against his car and stared off into space. His eyes and mind were tired. All he wanted to do was curl up next to Bridget in bed for a few blessed moments, though he knew she'd be leaving soon for her training classes. The final week they let them start a little later, but everyone was normally so wound up mentally, they didn't care.

Something moved near the side of her house and he was instantly alert. His hand went to where his holster would have been and he cursed. He might be over reacting, but he'd been damned certain a person had shifted in the shadows.

Slowly, Jeremy pushed himself off the car and started to walk toward the side of the house. As he turned the corner, he saw a man run down the street, passing by him so quickly that he was at a loss as to how to trap him.

He warred with himself, wanting to go after the man. Someone was spying on Bridget and it unnerved him. Granted, she was a fairly well known model for those who knew those things, it could have been paparazzi. The last thing he needed was an assault charge. He cracked his knuckles and let out a long sigh. He would leave this up to Bridget. The worst that could happen is she would be pissed he hadn't chased the man down.

His cell phone vibrated and he pulled it out of his pocket.

Come on in.

A smile eased across his face, replacing some of the nervous tension. It dissipated completely as he slipped the phone back into his jeans pocket. He hurried and walked around the front of the house. Jeremy's eyes widened as he turned the knob on the front door and it opened slowly.

"Sweet Jesus, Bridget. You're trying to kill me, aren't you, Darlin'?" his voice was immediately thick with desire.

She laughed, the whimsical sound one he loved so much, and tossed her head backward. A devious smile spread over her lips as her hips swayed as she literally sauntered over to him. He felt the blood rush to his dick, and his tongue felt swollen in his mouth as he thought about all the things he'd was going to be doing with it.

"I might be. Or I might have just been up early and slept in this."

His eyes trailed up and down her body, taking in the black silk and lace corset that pushed her perfect breasts higher, made them even more perfect. She wore a tiny scrap of a thong with a rhinestone bow at the top of it and black heels to match.

"Oh, right. I forgot, people think all southern men are stupid," he said playfully.

He took a step forward and wrapped a hand behind her head, pulling it up as he leaned down to kiss her. Their mouths fit together as if they were made for one another. Her small sigh of pleasure made him smile against her lips. He was more than ready to give her what she wanted, but his mind reminded him of what he'd seen moments ago. A frustrated groan escaped him as he drew himself back.

"Before I push you against that wall and show you exactly what that little number is making me think of doing, we need to talk."

She pouted her lips, and he felt his dick get even harder by the second.

"There was someone outside just now. Near the side of your house. When I walked up to him, he bolted." She frowned and he immediately kept talking and wondered if he shouldn't check out the rest of the place. "I thought he was a papa, but I didn't look to see if he had any equipment."

She looked down at the carpet for a moment and then back at him. "They have found me more than once. Models aren't always entertaining, but when you were as close to supermodel status as I was, well, you become much more interesting." Though she spoke the words, he wasn't convinced she believed them.

"Do you want me to have a look around? Make sure the creep or creeps aren't out there?"

She shook her head. "No, I'm certain it was just one trying to see if they'd found my home finally." She moved toward him, pulling the hem of his t-shirt up and over his head. "There are other things I'd like to do before I have to leave." She leaned up and kissed him, gently rocking her hips against his crotch.

"Mmm. Are there, Miss O'Casey?" He captured her mouth with his own and laved her tongue, with his while his hands massaging her firm breasts without unhooking the corset. "And just how many minutes do I have before you must leave?"

She grinned at him and unzipped his pants without hesitation. "About eighteen minutes. I suggest you use them wisely." As she was talking she pulled his pants down to his ankles, taking his briefs with them. Bridget looked up at him and smirked as she trailed her finger across the tip of his shaft, spreading the little bit of pre cum around it. "Looks like you're certainly speeding up the process."

Without another word, she sank to her knees and took him into her mouth. The sensation hit him so hard his knees almost buckled. He fisted his hands in her short hair, guiding her mouth as she sucked him.

Her tongue played over his dick, trailing behind her lips and increasing the delicious friction so much so his hips were bucking into her mouth before long. It drove him crazy. Every stroke of her tongue felt more sensual than the last. She was taking him so deeply with each thrust he was completely enveloped in the heat of her mouth. When she pulled back the cold air sent chills down his spine.

"Dear god, Darlin'. I'm not going to last much longer if you keep doing that."

Jeremy swore as he felt her grin against his cock. He felt her reach out to and gently massage his balls, even as her mouth slid his full length into her mouth. Stars sprang in front of his vision clouded as he felt his whole entire body tense. Her movements grew frantic. Jeremy's hands were guiding her head quicker, her sucks were harder and his hips were thrusting so quickly he couldn't stop himself as he came.

His body jerked as the rush of pleasure rippled across his body. She continued to suck, lick and torture him until she had wrung every last drop of pleasure from his body. He was buzzing with need, thinking he wouldn't be able to go another round after a release she'd given him like that even though he certainly wanted to.

Bridget let go of his balls and pulled her mouth off his dick. The lust in her eyes as she stood up. It ignited something in him and he crushed his mouth down onto hers.

She leaned against him, dizzy from the pleasure and the throbbing need of her own desire. Her body ached, eager to have him within her. She'd wanted to do something just for him this morning though. A little surprise simply because she could. With every suck on his cock she'd grown wetter and wetter, remembering just how good he felt inside of her.

As his mouth claimed hers she whimpered so loudly, she surprised herself.

"I can't promise you it will be nearly as amazing as that was, but it's my turn." His voice was husky, sensual and panty wetting.

The scandalous glint in his eye sent a wave of moisture to pool between her thighs and she didn't even try to argue with him. Jeremy picked her up and walked to the couch, she was shocked at how gently he laid her down before lowering himself down onto her body, and took off her thong with his damn teeth.

Bridget's legs squeezed together, she was trembling with need and trying to hurry the process along. She felt the hot wetness of his breath caress her aching mound and her hips bucked off the couch. His tongue slid along her slit and slipped inside without warning. Her entire body shot up, off the couch as pleasure licked through her veins. He pressed his big hands to her hips, holding her in and keeping her from shooting off the couch.

She was so close to the edge she was already seeing stars. He tasted her as if she was a fine wine that needed to be savored. Bridget's body squirmed beneath him. Her breathing grew shallow, slow and hitched, with every stroke of his tongue in and out of her core. She balled her hands into fists, thrusting her hips greedily trying to take more.

She came. Her screams reverberated throughout the room. Her entire body shook as he continued to lick at her until the spasms died down. He pushed himself onto his elbows once her body's release subsided and grinned at her and she laughed.

"I think we've had quite the successful morning, wouldn't you say?"

15

Trevor couldn't believe his luck. He growled to himself as he got onto the bus. Some giant of a man had pulled into Bridget's driveway at the exact moment he'd begun to get comfortable watching her. The way the man had moved, Trevor was certain he was law enforcement. Which meant she had either followed in Jimmy's footsteps and was a cop now, or she just had a daddy complex.

But it could ruin his plans. One man shouldn't be able to tear them apart but if he couldn't get to O'Casey's kid it wouldn't be enough for Trevor. They'd been so careful, there was no way that anything had could have been connected to anyone, let alone the daughter of a cop. So he assumed the man was simply been her boyfriend or whatever. For a moment, half a minute, he'd considered taking the guy on. But he'd learned a lot in lock up. The most important thing he'd learned in jail, however, was to not fight someone bigger than you. You'd wind up their bitch.

Trevor tapped his foot with impatience. It always tapped when he was thinking. There was no way in Hell he could include Bridget O'Casey in his plans if he had to go past the giant of a man that was sleeping with her.

"Which means you'll just have to leave her out."

Feeling angry again, he pulled out his phone and called Mikey.

"Yea, Trevor?"

"Any idea what Bridget O'Casey does for a living out here?"

"Umm, yea. I texted you like an hour ago. Figured you'd really enjoy that shit when you saw it."

Trevor squeezed the phone harder, wishing it was Mikey's neck for playing games. "Well, obviously I haven't, so talk."

"Found her in the database for the academy . . . the police academy."

Trevor laughed as his brain processed the news. A smile slid across his lips. He hung the phone up without uttering another word.

If Bridget O'Casey was at the department, it would make it so much easier to take her down. It removed the desire he had of sleeping with her first, but he got off just fine on ending police officers lives. Hers would be that much the sweeter.

Trevor chewed on his thumbnail and put the phone in his pocket as the bus pulled up to the curb. Bridget would fit into his plans perfectly. With everything mapped out, he didn't need to grab her to include her in what would come soon enough.

Two cars, two crews. They were going to box the cops into their own fucking parking lot and take as many down as they could before getting the hell out of there. It lacked the finesse of his other plans, but this one was about sheer numbers and timing to get Bridget included into the mix.

Sitting on the bus, his entire body hummed with energy. It would take another day to learn more about the academy's schedule. He preferred to get her when her boyfriend wasn't around, but before the end of the week, the entire LAPD was going to feel the pain of their brothers in arms around them.

By the end of the week, Travis would walk away, scot-free.

"Yes! I won. Marcus, where the hell are you, man? Get your hide up and over here! We beat the girls. Well, I beat the girl." Jeremy beamed down at Bridget with pride. "Come on, O'Casey, admit it. Guys are the better shot after all."

Bridget glared up at him from her position on the ground. "I don't know why the fuck they let you come back and partner up." she growled as she looked at the mark on her shirt, the fatal simulation wound.

He gave her that deviously sexy side smirk of his. Bridget was torn between wanting to slap it off his face, and wanting to take him some place a little more private.

"Because, cops have the option to take part in the final simulation battleground, firing training."

"Yes, but I don't understand why they let *you* do it."

When he'd shown up that morning and announced he'd be participating, she'd been thrilled. All she'd wanted to do was show his ass up. Now, she was more than a tad grumpy they'd let him play.

"Hey, it's barely been two weeks since I was a cop and I am a consultant until further notice. So, Chase really had no option but to let me play." His tone of voice was so cocky and she wished it hadn't also sounded so sexy because of his stupid accent.

She was still lying in on the ground, with bark of some sort digging into her arms, not to mention probably sticking to her training clothes, and he had the nerve to be so damn sexy. She couldn't deny that he'd turned her on. Jeremy extended a hand to help her up. She lifted her chin defiantly and ignored it, pushing herself to her knees and promptly standing up.

Her eyes locked with his when she once she'd finished brushing some of the dirt off. "Ok, fine, Trellins, boys are better….at simunition shootings."

She gave him a smirk of her own. He shook his head and chuckled.

Still laughing, Jeremy shrugged good naturedly. "Better than nothing, Darlin'."

A playful light danced within his blue eyes. He looked a complete and total mess. His short chestnut brown hair was mussed and his bronzed arms were covered in paint splatters from the non-fatal hits he'd taken throughout the course. One of which had come from her. Yet his smile was still utterly perfect. As they turned to exit the small simulation course set up outside the building, Marcus rounded the corner. His still to long white-blond hair hung loose around his shoulders and he was grinning, almost as if he'd heard Jeremy shout through the building and that was impossible.

"Ahh, I feel so much better after a shower. The one benefit of having a lousy shot compared to you two is I get to shower earlier. The only problem with it is the damn locker room was crowded because of how fast you two fucking shoot people. Oh, and I passed by the way. Apparently, this was more fun for you two." Marcus looked to Jeremy. "Who won?"

Jeremy grinned. Bridget opened her mouth, ready to make a comment. Marcus high-fived Jeremy. She glared at him instead and crossed her arms over her chest. She kind of hated him for being clean, too. She could feel whatever was in the shot starting to cake on her skin and she had enough dirt and sweat on her to turn anyone off.

"I just saw Ashley walking in. I'm shocked she lasted so long with you two. You know, O'Casey, you really should help her more with the no getting shot thing. You two could have won this as a team."

"Thanks for the tip, Marcus. I'll have to remember to tell Jeremy to look out for his next partner better than he did you."

She smirked and Marcus jokingly put a hand to his chest and stumbled backward.

"Oh, how your words inflict so much pain." he said, melodramatically and then smiled. "You should hit the showers too O'Casey. You're not looking like your supermodel self." Marcus teased and backed away as he saw her lift her arm in a playful swing.

"Shut up. He looks just as bad as I do." She jerked her thumb in Jeremy's direction.

She laughed when she caught sight of him. He did indeed look just as bad as she assumed she did.

Marcus was only playing about the supermodel comment but it still stung a little. They'd all grown to respect her enough that the little jab shouldn't have bothered her. Knowing that so many people would look her in a uniform and not take her seriously still ruffled her feathers. If not for her expert shot, people would have taken a lot longer to take her seriously in the academy, too. The fact that she'd been a cop's kid gave her a little credibility, but it was her shooting that had gotten her the most respect.

Before anyone else could get in a good natured rib, Chase walked up to the trio. "Good work, O'Casey. I'll be lying if I didn't say I'm upset Trellins got the best of you. But to be fair, you've only had a few months at this. If the DEA gives him a day off, I know I'd pay to watch a rematch."

She smiled at him and stuck her tongue out at Jeremy, even if it was immature. "Thank you, sir. I did get in a shot on him, thankfully. That should shut him up for a little bit."

Jeremy placed a quick kiss on her forehead. "That's what you think. I still killed you."

"Hey, watch that unprofessional shit on my watch." Chase raised a brow at them and tsked. "You'd best clean up after such a blow, Miss O'Casey. It looks like you took quite a few superficial hits, too."

"She sure did. But I was the one that finally took her down."

She looked at Jeremy like he was making her sick and couldn't help laughing at the gigantic smile on his lips. "Lord, that male ego on you southern boys certainly is something."

They all laughed. Chase playfully slapped Jeremy across his back. "Seeing as how you've shot at real perps, it would have been embarrassing for you had you not. Don't listen to him, O'Casey. Danvers hates cocky cops. Probably why he was so damned happy to pass this fool off to the DEA."

Jeremy's grin grew wider.

"All right, as I'm sure you were told, this was really just for fun. Congratulations, kid. As of a few hours ago, you officially passed your final entrance exam to the LAPD. Your session with Annalisse showed nothing unstable to match that outburst of yours."

She felt like her heart was going to beat of her chest. She'd finally finished. It had taken her father's death to give her the push she'd truly needed, but now she was able to do good, and in his name, too. She knew a huge smile had spread across her face. She could barely contain the desire to shout and tackle

Jeremy in the process, so the smile would just have to stay.

"Thank you, sir. It's been an honor to train under you."

Chase laughed and pointed at Jeremy who looked steamed. "Might want to watch the wording before Trellins' pops a blood vessel or something, but it's been my pleasure. Now, you two, hit the showers and head out. Early day today. You're expected back on Monday at 0600 hours to get your first official schedule and meet your partners."

"Why? What's up, Chase? We always have a little pizza party for the recruits after the game. What gives?"

Jeremy just couldn't keep his mouth shut ever she was learning, but it did make her curious. Plus, she couldn't totally hate that part about him since if he hadn't bought her a drink when they'd first met, she wouldn't be as happy as she was with him in her life right now.

Chase looked back and forth between the three of them. Bridget's hackles rose with apprehension, automatically not liking where this was going. Chase cleared his throat and did his best to make eye contact only with Jeremy when he started talking.

"A cop, Sanders, was shot today. About three hours ago when the simunition course began. Luckily, his partner intervened. He's in the hospital in pretty bad shape, but we're told he will make it. We're going to go check in on him in a few hours, give him some more personal time. In light of everything that's been going on, well, Danvers isn't convinced this isn't connected to everything, so we're running on a skeleton crew."

Bridget gasped, sucking in air through her nose because her mouth was shut. Marcus shifted uncomfortably from foot to foot, seeming to have already known and Jeremy let out a low curse. She hated that people were going after law enforcement like this. She hated that they were no closer to apprehending the perpetrators. A part of her was too disgusted to even comprehend that it had happened right in their own county, in the LAPD. Another part of her had enough sense to grasp onto the words with concern. She'd soon be an official a member of the LAPD in a few short days. They were going to be thrust into a world more dangerous than they had ever known because before the attacks had never been truly against them.

"Is there any chance they caught the people?" Her voice shook and she wished she had a modicum of control over it, but she didn't and Chase didn't seem to notice her weakness.

"We did. There's no way of knowing if this guy is connected to the bigger picture. However, we do have a small problem. Bridget, this could have been connected to your father."

Bridget's face paled. Her body swayed beneath the onslaught of his words. She wasn't certain whether she moved, or if Jeremy had simply stepped up to stand behind her. Either way, her body slammed into his. Jeremy's arms slid around her, holding her tightly against him. For a moment, the sky and ground seemed to merge together. The feel of Jeremy's body against hers was the only thing that kept her rooted in place.

"How so, Chase?" Jeremy asked, the sound of his voice vibrating through every inch of her body and she was grateful he was there to ask the question she couldn't force out.

"The guy that shot Sanders, we nailed him. His name was Mikey Tallenfo. A while back, your dad was a part of a bust that interrupted a gang committing armed robberies across the whole of Southern California. Two of the men were put behind bars. One for murder, and one named by the others for protection as the leader. Tallenfo was one of the ones not prosecuted. Now I'm wondering if that was a mistake."

"Son of a bitch. It can't be, can it?" Jeremy asked.

"Can't be what?" Marcus prodded, a slight frown marring his forehead.

She was as confused as Marcus one moment, and then the next, she just wasn't. "You think these guys are attacking all of the departments that had a hand in the bust?"

Chase nodded, the look on his face grim. "That's exactly what we think, which could possibly put you in harm's way, O'Casey. Ah, don't say anything, Trellins. She's got two patrol cars sitting outside her house already, and Ashley's jeep was checked for bombs the minute the connection was made since they drove in together."

"None of that matters. I won't be leaving her side."

Chase scoffed at his words. Bridget's heart swelled with pride, thankful of the fact that Jeremy was adamant in protecting her. She took a deep breath, hoping to calm the sudden dizziness she felt. Pulling herself away from Jeremy, she realized she needed to be strong enough to do things on her own. She'd make a terrible cop if she kept relying on him whenever things went awry.

Bridget thought back to the man Jeremy had seen sneaking around her house. Dread pooled in the pit of her stomach at the thought of the vile killer being close enough to spy on her and she'd been oblivious. How could she have not known?

"So, they think this is all revenge? And now that you have one of them it may be possible to bring them all in?"

271

"Watch the hopeful tone, O'Casey. It's a long stretch. But yes, that's exactly what we are hoping. This is going to sound moronic and impossible, but don't dwell on it. Get washed up and head home. We're going to be doing everything we can to end this. Tonight. It's gone on long enough, and no more police need to be attacked this way. Not if we're right about the connection."

She nodded and sighed. Jeremy slipped his hand into hers.

"I think this once they'll make an exception for inappropriate conduct. Plus, you were just dismissed for the day."

Bridget offered him a weak smile. "Marcus, do you think you and Ashley could wait for me? If we're going to have to pretend to be normal, we should grab happy hour somewhere."

"Sure thing. I'll go let her know, and we'll wait in the lot. You two better do a good job of scrubbing up if we're going to celebrate." His tone was stressed, although she could tell he was trying to sound happy, for her sake.

Marcus headed back into the building and went took a left, while she and Jeremy walked right, heading for the showers.

Bridget couldn't help but notice how empty the halls were. They passed two other recruits but there were so few officers remaining. Which meant someone really was nervous about the LAPD being next on the hit list.

She passed a mirror, just outside the entrance to the locker room and took a good look at herself. Her dark black hair was falling out of its tiny bun, in wisps curling in every which direction. The brown in her Bridget's brown eyes was a darker shade than normal. Her sun-kissed skin was indeed splattered with dirt and flecks of paint and it was also all over her face. It did nothing to shatter her flawless image. Nor could it, the fact remained that she was still a model who'd trained to be a cop. The woman in the mirror She was still striking as always, with her dark hair and large, bright eyes, and skin that was still blissfully tan; thanks to her mother's Hispanic background working against her father's Irish one.

Bridget had secretly thought that when she looked at herself on the day she graduated the police academy that she wouldn't see some fashion model in a costume. That she would see a hard, tough, female cop.

She felt Jeremy nudge her shoulder. She looked away from the mirror, her cheeks flushed with color.

"What's wrong, Darlin'? Is this all too much for you?"

The concern in his voice broke the little that remained of her self control. Several tears slid down her cheeks and Bridget wiped them away with a quick flick of her hand.

"Would you think less of me if I said yes?" She finally said after a period of silence.

Jeremy took a step toward her and tugged her against his chest. He tilted her head up, and brushed his lips across hers. His kiss was soft, gentle and comforting. It was everything she needed it and him to be right now. She let herself forget where they were and what they were told, enjoying the moment they shared between them. She was beautiful to him and she could be thankful he saw something in her, even if all she could see in herself was a model. It did wonders to erase the blunt darkness of Chase's revelation.

His hands trailed down her back, and she found herself leaning closer into him. Bridget caught herself at the last moment and, pulled herself back from the kiss.

"Do you realize where we are?" her voice was husky with need and she was shocked it had happened so quickly.

Jeremy chuckled and ran a finger down her arm before placing a kiss on the lower right side of her neck, a place he knew she loved. She shivered, causing him to do it once more.

"Darlin', there is no way this would go any further than this. You simply looked like you needed it. Needed someone to remind you that you're right here and still alive. I'll keep doing that for you, you know that, right?"

She felt her lips tremble at his admission. Taking a deep breath, she smiled and smiling at him.

Everything with them had started off as wrong as it possibly could have. A one-night stand that had turned into a failed relationship upon learning they'd be subordinates here at work to falling into bed together. And now , now, they had a real relationship. One that she never wanted to let go of. Ever.

"Jeremy?"

Concern flickered in the depths of his eyes again. He pressed a gentle kiss to her lips and promptly pulled himself back.

"Yes?"

"I don't want to scare you off or anything, but I'm in love with you."

Bridget held her breath, not knowing what to expect once the words were out. Despite everything, they hadn't said such words to one another before. She couldn't help but to wonder if he felt the same way she did.

The smile on his face chased away her fears. The sexy little side smirk that drove her mad was quickly on his face. He held her against him before capturing her lips again. This time, the kiss was deep, hungry almost. She felt her body pulse and heard him moan just as he pulled himself away.

"Jesus, Bridget, I love you, too." He kissed her again and when she tried to wrap her arms around his neck, he took a step back. "I love you so damn much, I'm not going to let us do something stupid and ruin your career. Go shower. I'll see you out in the lot, and while you're in there, think about me." He winked at her.

She chewed on her lower lip, aching to throw herself into his arms again. Bridget knew he was doing the right thing. *Just breathe and walk into the locker room,* she told herself as she turned to push the door open but stopped for a moment.

"Oh, and Jeremy," she said, pausing momentarily. "You might want to follow my lead and shower."

She winked at him. He scoffed at her and pushed the door to the men's locker room open. Bridget headed inside to find the locker room was empty. The environment felt a little eerie. Though she was the last of the recruits, she'd assumed some of them might still be around cleaning up.

Her brow furrowed as she thought about Ashley "When was the last time you saw Ashley?" She was talking to herself as she pulled the soiled cotton top off over her head.

Marcus had seen her walking out of the showers recently but Marcus's words irked her now. The fact that she hadn't seen Ashley for almost thirty minutes before Jeremy took her down made her feel smug just for a moment. Then, she remembered that shooting wasn't enough to keep each other safe. It wasn't keeping cops around Southern California safe at present either.

Bridget tried to force her mind to go blank as she squirmed out of the nylon shorts she wore. She walked over to the nearest shower and turned on the water. The hiss as the water came out made her twitch. For the second time that day, she thought about how unnerving it was to be alone right now. She picked the end shower and quickly looked down the row of lockers and stalls to confirm she truly was alone before hurrying into the last shower stall and stepping under the cool spray.

Jeremy couldn't ignore how hot it was outside for December, drops of water were stuck to his skin. He'd rushed through his shower, afraid of leaving Bridget alone too long. If he hadn't, he might have ended up taking a little too much personal time in the showers. Plus a few others had been in there. With others in the room, it was something he didn't need to be doing no matter how turned on their brief kisses had gotten him. He preferred to wait for her in the hallway instead.

The look she'd given herself when she'd looked in the mirror worried him. But what had come next? He'd loved that. He was still buzzing on a high from the fact that she loved him, and loved him enough to say it first. Everything about Bridget had screamed perfection from the moment he'd met her. Nothing had changed that. She was everything he'd ever wanted in a woman and probably a million things more. Knowing that there was a shot that one day he'd come home from work to her sitting on the couch sipping a glass of wine or laying in bed with a book was enough to demand he do everything in his power to keep her safe.

His mind raced as he thought about the recent events taking place at the various precincts. He'd known Sanders and was upset as Hell that the guy had been shot badly enough to be in in critical condition. Though, it had been nothing compared to what he had felt when Chase had said the killers might have had motive to come after Bridget personally.

He was restless standing in the hall and grabbed his phone from his pocket and sent her a quick text that he would meet her in the lot. He just had too much energy to stand still with everything that had gone on.

A low growl slid past his lips as he pushed open the door leading to the lot. His eyes scanned the lot, looking for Ashley's annoyingly bright Jeep. When he didn't see it right away he walked further to the left and spotted it parked facing the street and in the row closest to the road – they must have gotten in late this morning if they'd parked so far from the building.

From his vantage point he saw Ashley pulling her corn silk yellow hair into some sort of a knot on her head. Marcus lounged happily in the backseat. He stood there debating going in to walk her out but remembered his text saying they would just meet in the lot. The last thing he wanted to do was make her feel more fragile than she already felt. He jogged over to the car, and felt a bead of sweat slip down his neck.

"So much for that cold shower. Fucking hot winters." He missed the cool weather of the Midwest this time of year.

"So, Marcus tells me that we're doing happy hour to celebrate. Does that mean the veteran buys?" Ashley asked with a wink when he got up to the car.

Jeremy chuckled and looked anxiously behind him for Bridget. "Sure, why not? I've got a big flashy salary now." He grinned and they both laughed. He looked at Marcus, "swap me seats so I can whisper how wonderful Bridget is into her ear once she gets here." The words were playful, but the truth was he wanted to hold her after what they'd learned.

His grin broadened and he climbed over the back gate to slide into the back seat. The sight of the parking lot being so empty unnerved him. He realized that Ashley hadn't been there when Chase had told them the news.

"In all seriousness, did you tell her, Marcus?"

"Tell me what?"

He sighed. The last thing he wanted was to potentially be explaining this to Ashley and have Bridget walk out of the building.

"They have a possible connection between today's shooting and the county shootings."

Ashley's eyes widened with horror as she turned to face Marcus. "What? Marcus, why would you forget to tell me that? Especially after the scare with my brother."

Jeremy sighed and closed his eyes for a moment. "I'm not done, Ashley. There's a possible tie between this and a crime spree that was busted in large part by Bridget's dad a few years back. Which means–"

Ashley cut him off. "She could be in danger."

He nodded. "Exactly. She could be, but she isn't because I have no intention of letting anyone touch her. I just wanted to make sure you were aware of what was going on." Jeremy looked down at his watch. "Jesus, sometimes I wonder if she ever remembers how to get ready without a team of stylists. She went into the locker room almost twenty-six minutes ago."

Jeremy was twitchy. With all the "what ifs" rolling around inside his head the last thing he wanted was for the woman he loved to be in danger. The idea of loving Bridget smoothed over him and soothed the ander and uncertainty he felt inside of him a little. There was so much that they had a lot to look forward to together once the perpetrators of this hideous crime spree were caught.

Ashley laughed. "Lost in your own mind?"

He raised a brow at her and felt his face grow warm. "Sorry, I was thinking about Bridget. Not to sound like less of a man, but she's pretty fucking perfect. I can't think of a time when I didn't get to say that out loud. I don't want to go anywhere but straight ahead with her." He sounded like such a sap, but he didn't even care.

Ashley cooed with delight. He saw Marcus roll his eyes in the rear-view mirror and turned around to face him.

"I'm sure she'll be out in a little bit. Girls do take a little longer to dry."

Ashley laughed, poking the wet bun on the top of her head with a fingertip.

"You know what the best part of dating a cop is?" Ashley and Marcus turned and looked at him. "That she can kick my ass anytime. I don't have to treat her like she's some damsel in distress."

They all laughed. The conversation switched easily into getting ready for the next week and what it would mean. Christmas was in four days. His job at the DEA would start soon after. If he had to jump back on the force to carry a gun to take down those likely to threaten Bridget, he would do it.

Jeremy was so lost deep within his thoughts he barely heard Ashley and Marcus carrying on in the front seat like two bratty siblings. Nor did he notice the black Mercedes SLK that pulled into the lot and drive past Ashley's Wrangler before finding a spot near the entrance. He also failed to see the men sliding open the doors leading into the precinct.

16

Nothing quite like a cool shower, Bridget thought as she turned off the water. Stepping out of the shower stall, she grabbed the towel and dried herself off as quickly as possible and saw her clothes on the bench.

"Nothing like having to put on dirty clothes after. she said with a groan.

She shuddered and silently cursed herself for not leaving an extra pair of clothes in the locker for situations like this. "Yes, because shootings happen and police stations close down so fucking often."

The problem was, police brutality was becoming more and more common. She tugged her shirt on over her head and sighed.

The shower had done a little to close her mind off to all the thoughts Chase had put there. From the shootings to her potential danger, and now it was all rushing back at her as the isolation from standing in the shower was gone.

She took a deep breath once she'd pulled her shorts on and stared at her reflection in the mirror again, as if something could have changed during the short shower.

"Still the same old Bridget. Even when you're practically a cop, you're still being guarded by them." Bridget hadn't meant for the comment to sound as bitter as it did in the empty locker room.

It was the truth. She was officially now a member of the LAPD, well would be next week at least. Plus, she was about to go home to a house guarded by patrol cars until further notice.

She wished she had something she could protect herself with, but they'd only been using training guns that they checked out of the arms locker and had to check back in when everything was done. She was a cops daughter, but that didn't mean she randomly kept guns when she was strutting half naked as a model.

"Maybe I could just stop by andask about the policy."

Her mind raced as she thought about her options. The idea sounded ridiculous, even to her ears but it didn't stop her from walking out of the locker room and head for the front desk.

Luckily, Lieutenant Parsons was still on and the older woman gave her a gentle smile.

"Miss O'Casey, what brings you here after your completion of course?"

She took a deep breath to steady herself and said, "I was wondering– in the instance of being a potential target and one of the newest sets of LAPD personnel," her voice trailed off and she sighed. She felt like she was four-years-old asking to have a cookie before dinner. "Could I check out a gun? Would that be possible to do? Just until mine is issued to me next week."

Parsons shook her head, slowly and the partially grey strands of hair whipped behind her head. "Sorry, O'Casey. That's completely a no."

That's when Bridget heard it, when they both heard it based on Parsons twitch. A gunshot erupted somewhere in the building. Their eyes locked almost instantly on one another, panic lurking in their depths. Bridget felt her heart begin to beat so rapidly she could scarcely hear anything but her heartbeat. There was no mistaking that sound. A trained person would recognize it even in their sleep and fortunately, or unfortunately, they were both trained.

Parsons turned and grabbed a gun from the locked unit behind her. Bridget almost missed the woman move. She tossed a gun in Bridget's direction. Bridget caught it within her hands, and checked the gun's magazine.

"Take it. If that was what we both fear it was I'm not sending you out unarmed. I'd rather you stay here completely but I know that look. I've seen it in the eyes of more than one police officer. I'll deal with the paperwork. You just make sure you're out of harm's way and that's just for protection."

Another shot rang out and Bridget wasn't certain if she was actually reaching forward for the gun or standing frozen in place. Not until her hand wrapped around it and her index finger flicked the gun's safety off. Panic seized her. She couldn't force her feet to move, no matter how much her mind screamed for her to do so. She couldn't wait any longer and she couldn't seem to move either. Suddenly, with the sound of yet another shot going off nearby penetrated the slight fog inside her head. Her feet finally got the message.

Thoughts of Jeremy and the others were running rampant through her head. They were waiting for her outside the entire time. Bridget was unsure as to whether those shots had come from inside or outside. Refusing to wait another second, she ran. Her feet slammed down the empty hallway echoing behind her. She could hear several on duty officers shouting orders to one another as they ran, most likely, toward the source of the shots.

She stopped dumbfounded as she saw three men, including Chase, head out the front door. Another three sped past her as well. Six were headed toward the door leading to the lot. Without thinking, she sprinted past them. Bridget knew there were protocols to take into consideration, but all she could think about was the people she'd known were outside. She was breaking every fucking rule.

But she didn't care.

All she could think of was Jeremy lying in a pool of his own blood, just as her father must have been not too long ago. She burst into the lot, unable to focus on anything as the image began to take hold of her ability to focus on anything else. She felt bile rising up in her throat as she looked around. Two officers lay on the ground. Dead or alive, she couldn't tell. Her feet were running as fast as she could force them to move and her chest burned from the effort.

Less than ten feet from her was Ashley's Wrangler. She couldn't breathe as her eyes took in everything in front of her. Blood was splattered on the driver's side door. A man lay, dressed in all black, unmoving on the side of the car with a bullet hole in his head.

Bridget didn't waste any time on him. She turned towards the vehicle, her breath catching as she saw that Ashley was slumped over the steering wheel. Bridget couldn't see any sign of blood or any indication as to where her closest friend had been shot. She couldn't see any sign of movement either.

That's when she caught Marcus stumbling out of the corner of her eye. He was standing just outside the car with his gun drawn, aiming it directly at the window of another car, and Bridget had no idea why. It didn't matter where he aimed it though. Just like in the earlier simulation course he didn't watch every angle. An unexpected bullet shattered through the driver's window and out Ashley's passenger side window as a car pulled up behind them. It slammed into Marcus, lodging itself directly into his back, right between his shoulder blades. Bridget watched as a bright red flower formed and quickly spread out. Without uttering a single sound, Marcus' body fell forward and slammed into the ground.

Bridget's own cry tore through the lot. She could hear the other officer's screams as they ran forward to surround the Mercedes and the Honda Accord that clearly didn't belong in the lot. She couldn't make herself focus on anything but Marcus' lifeless form laying on the ground like a limp doll encircled by his own blood.

Rage tore through her as she watched the scene. No one was shooting at her, not at that moment. Just then a man appeared to her left, as if out of thin air. He wasn't the scrawniest man in the world and he wasn't terribly intimidating either. She couldn't see his face of the black beanie he wore tugged down that covered everything but his eyes. Seeing his eyes was like a bucket of ice water dumping over her head, just for a second. The dead look in his eyes frightened her. Grey pools of nothing surrounded an iris and they were focused on her.

"Bridget O'Casey," he said. "I've been thinking about this for days, little O'Casey. I wanted to take you, fuck you nice and slow. But now that I know you're a cop too, that won't be happening. How about you do me a favor and just say hello to papa O'Casey? Tell him from Trevor sent you. You'll be getting a one way ticket to see him."

Bridget stood there, rooted in place. Anger coursed through her unlike anything she had ever felt before. She had no idea who the man was but her anger boiled beneath the surface at the mention of her father. She knew, then, that the killings at the various precincts were at his words. This had all been connected to her. Chase had been right after all.

There would have been some consequence of shooting first and asking questions later when dealing with a person in charge of such diabolical crimes. But she didn't care. The mention of her father rang in her ears. Her anger flared anew. She refused to let this man rip apart her entire world. Somehow, some way, she'd make him pay, no matter the consequences.

Bridget took aim at him, even as he walked in her direction, his own gun pointed at her. It felt like an eternity passed as she waited for her finger to push the trigger back far enough to send a bullet flying at the man just in front of Ashley's Jeep.

Her aim was perfect and her shot was quicker than this Trevor man's was. It slammed into the center of his forehead, and his gun flew into the air before he got a chance to fire it.

He dropped to the ground like a sack filled with stones. She gagged as she saw the blood trickle out of his head and down his face. Consumed by rage, she fired a second bullet into his chest, ensuring that he wouldn't get up ever again.

Bridget's chest heaved as she stood over him. Everything around her had gone quiet. Her heart ached as she tried to make sense of what she'd done. She couldn't hear the other officers or the bullets still flying because the attack wasn't over.

She'd never killed anyone before.

Tears blurred her vision and the world began to blur and spin around her. She doubled over as bile crept up her throat and she began to hyperventilate. Jeremy.

"Bridget!" a voice cried, penetrating the walls of the fog that seemed to cloud her mind. "Bridget, get the fuck back!"

She straightened and turned away from the dead body to see Jeremy running toward her, shouting something she couldn't quite hear. He was ok, somehow he wasn't lying dead in the Wrangler with Ashley.

But he didn't have a gun. Anger and fear were etched across every inch of his face. She almost dropped her own weapon and ran to him. She wanted nothing more than to feel his arms around her again.

Bridget caught sight of two men dressed in black racing toward Jeremy.

Before she could react, could scream his name and tell him to get out of the way, she saw his body pitch forward, but didn't hit the ground, as a bullet slammed into the back of his right shoulder. Another sprayed blood from his lower back.

"No!" She wasn't sure how long she screamed the word for.

She lifted her arm and her finger slammed the trigger down three times. All three shots hit their targets. One slammed deep into the gut of the man that had just shot Jeremy. Time had hardly moved but it felt as if everything was trickling by in slow motion.

"Move, move, move." She wasn't sure if the police had shouted that, or the assailants.

"Trevor's down, come on, let's get the fuck out of here!" She knew that had to be one of the men working for the man she'd killed first.

Her eyes were on Jeremy's as he looked at hers, pain and fear mixing with tears in his eyes. She felt the gun slip from her fingers. She dove after it, to cover Jeremy. But she heard a lone gun shot ring out. Her eyes darted up, just in time to see Jeremy grab his stomach and crash sideways to the ground.

Bridget stopped breathing. She watched as two men scrambled into the Mercedes, and heard the peel out of tires, echoing through the parking lot, presumably the other car because there had been too many men to have come out of a two-seater with a tiny trunk.

She froze, unsure of what to do. To rush to Jeremy, to ensure he was ok. Or to do what she was trained to do. Tears spilled down her face as her focus remained on the man she'd just said "I love you too." to. He wasn't moving and staring at him wasn't going to change that.

"O'Casey, get the fuck back." a voice ordered but she didn't.

Fury rippled through every inch of her body, gripped her every sense as her mind pieced together the longest three minutes of her life. Her senses that told her to be rational, that she should and listen to what she was being told. The injured needed to be checked to see if they were alive or dead. Yet she couldn't to let go of the rage building within her by the second. She was devoured by pain and anger and her actions were not logical. They weren't hers to control, they were lost to the rage.

The Mercedes lurched to life and Bridget grabbed the gun off the concrete and opened fire. She aimed at the spinning tires, missing her mark. Her aim was off because her brain wasn't focused, it couldn't be focused right now. The car sped over the planter and out onto the street.

She had no recollection of bolting through the lot and hopping over the small bump of the sidewalk to chase after the car. It swerved to avoid the Los Angeles afternoon traffic, trying to get away from the horrific crime scene.

Her mind went blank as she aimed her gun once more and fired, doing her best to run alongside to stop them. She saw nothing but her most recent memories.

She remembered seeing that damn Jeep, her friend's inert form bent over the steering wheel. Seeing Ashley it in before she'd even had a chance to protect her academy partner. She remembered Marcus's body blossoming with red and crashing to the ground. She remembered the determined look in Jeremy's eyes as he'd ran toward her. He'd wanted to protect her, as he took bullets he couldn't defend himself from.

It was burned into her mind. Every moment of it.

The memories, as bad as they were, kept her from dropping to her knees on the sidewalk and falling apart. Her mind seemed to register her surroundings, and she saw someone jump out of the vehicle when they couldn't force the car through traffic.

She gasped as she felt cold metal pierce her skin sending. The icy cold pain that was metal hitting warm blood felt like nothing she'd ever known. She felt it each time, each bullet as it ripped into her body. One in her leg and another in her stomach. The impact slowed her down and red clouded her vision. Pain leapt through her like fire and she felt the last shot. Her breath was knocked from her lungs as a bullet sunk into her chest.

There was no more running. No more simunition simulation training. Bridget felt herself connect with the sidewalk. Felt it as her head slammed into the ground, further jarring her body.

Bridget lay there and could feel the sticky liquid pool around her. She could feel it touching every part of her body outside where it had once touched her on the inside. She could almost feel the running footsteps of cops that raced in her direction, or maybe it was her imagination.

The she felt nothing, heard nothing and saw nothing.

"You have the right to remain silent when questioned. Anything you say or do may be used against you in a court of law." Bridget spoke the words with more conviction than she had intended to as she angrily slapped cuffs on her target. "Knowing and understanding your rights as I have explained them to you, are you willing to answer my questions without an attorney present?"

The man pressed into the ground gave a mumble of confirmation. She pulled her knee off his lower back and let him up, shoving him towards her partner as she did so.

"Think that about covers everything."

"You're certainly proving to be worth it in every way as a partner, O'Casey," Santana said, and gave her a small smile.

Tears pricked her eyes, as they had done every time Santana had said something sweet to her. Two months had passed since she'd nearly been killed outside in the precinct's parking lot. Two months of recovery, –both mentally and emotionally. Two months of learning how to live life without everyone she had lost that day. Without ever knowing what it would be like to serve with them. Without knowing what it would have been like to spend her life with Jeremy.

She'd been assigned to Santana the minute she'd demanded to be put back on rotation. No one had argued. Not Chase, not Danvers and not even Santana, who had every reason not to want a bad luck rookie by his side.

Whoever had figured out the connection, or supposed connection had been right. When she'd woken up a day and a half later in the ICU, Santana and Chase had been by her side, along with her mother and Danvers. Trevor Dennison had been a man her father had personally cuffed and locked up a little over five years ago. The name had sent a chill down her spine upon learning it. Though, she didn't feel guilty for killing him.

The only thing that had made it better was learning she'd been the one to take him down. She took pleasure in the fact that. Even if her mother voiced her displeasure with what Bridget had done.

They'd caught the others, thanks to her shooting the wheels and slowing them down. Learning the rest of the details about what had happened that day had nearly sent her back into a coma. It had been a week before she'd been anything more than a zombie, only eating and drinking when the hospital staff put something down in front of her.

Nothing would ever undo what she'd lost that day.

Her hand dipped inside her pocket. Bridget nodded at Santana as she wrapped her fingers around the small wallet she carried in her back pocket. Tears brimmed in her eyes and it was only a matter of

moments before Santana would catch her crying.
Again.

Bridget heard the patrol car door open and close
and she squeezed her eyes shut, not caring as the hot
tears tracked down her cheeks. With her eyes still
closed, she opened her wallet and pulled out the photo
of Jeremy, the one that she would always carry with
her now.

She opened her eyes and rubbed her fingers over
it. The paper was already wearing thin from her doing
so every time she thought of him. More tears coursed
down her face. Bridget shook her head, trying to clear
her eyes as she opened them and looked down at the
picture of the only man she'd ever loved. At the
second man who'd been taken from her because he'd
been a cop in the wrong place.

Bridget's eyes squeezed tightly shut and she
allowed herself to feel the pain all over again. Every
ounce of it washed over her as she thought about
Jeremy. In her mind, she saw that stupid side smirk of
his that could turn her knees to jelly. The fierce

protectiveness that shone in his eyes the day he lost his life flashed vividly through her mind.

"I'm doing this for you, Jeremy. For you and my dad." she whispered as she stood on the sidewalk of the little neighborhood they were in. Her voice trembled and tears slipped into her mouth. "I love you, Jeremy Trellins. I will always love you."

Taking a deep breath, she forced herself to open her eyes. With quick flicks of her hands, she slid the picture back into the viewing space where her ID should have been in Jeremy's wallet. Her wallet now.

"You'll always be with me, Jeremy. Always."

Bridget wiped the tears off her face and turned around. Santana's eyes were focused on her. He nodded his head, his way of telling her he understood. She took a deep breath to steady herself and walked back to the patrol car. They had a piece of scum to take in.

Made in the USA
Lexington, KY
02 February 2018